## "I need you to pretend to be madly in love with me."

Startled by the request, Dr. Blake Di Angelo tapped his thumbs against the sleek surface of his mahogany desk, thinking that perhaps the petite blonde pacing around his office had gone mad.

"You'll have to repeat that, Darby." He leaned against his leather chair's backrest, eyeing her with more than a little curiosity. "Because I don't think I heard you right."

She tossed an embossed card onto his desk and shuddered.

Blake picked up the card and studied the fancy maroon and gold embossing more closely. *Armadillo Lake Ten-Year High-School Reunion.*

Blake grinned. His eyes traveled over Darby's curvy little frame encased in a no-nonsense navy business suit, exposing shapely legs beneath her skirt hem. The shirt was tucked into a waist that his hands would probably fit around. He knew better than to let his thoughts go there.

Panic brewing in its blue depths, her gaze bored into him. "I really don't need the headache of looking for a date who'll no doubt get the wrong idea. But I do need a man for that weekend." Taking a deep breath, she lifted her shoulders and took on the expression of a seasoned soldier readying for battle. "And you're it."

**Janice Lynn** has a Master's in Nursing from Vanderbilt University, and works as a nurse practitioner in a family practice. She lives in the southern United States with her husband, their four children, their Jack Russell—appropriately named Trouble—and a lot of unnamed dust bunnies that have moved in since she started her writing career. To find out more about Janice and her writing, visit www.janicelynn.com

**Recent titles by the same author:**

PLAYBOY SURGEON, TOP-NOTCH DAD
THE PLAYBOY DOCTOR CLAIMS HIS BRIDE
SURGEON BOSS, SURPRISE DAD
THE NURSE'S BABY MIRACLE

# DR DI ANGELO'S BABY BOMBSHELL

### BY
### JANICE LYNN

First published in Great Britain 2010
Large Print edition 2010
Harlequin Mills & Boon Limited,
Eton House, 18-24 Paradise Road,
Richmond, Surrey TW9 1SR

© Janice Lynn 2010

ISBN: 978 0 263 21120 7

Harlequin Mills & Boon policy is to use papers that are
natural, renewable and recyclable products and made
from wood grown in sustainable forests. The logging and
manufacturing process conform to the legal environmental
regulations of the country of origin.

Printed and bound in Great Britain
by CPI Antony Rowe, Chippenham, Wiltshire

# DR DI ANGELO'S BABY BOMBSHELL

To Anna Sugden—
true friends are precious treasures
and you're a jewel that sparkles brightly
in my life. Thank you for the years of
laughter, shared tears, and unfailing support.
Love you!

# CHAPTER ONE

"I NEED you to pretend to be madly in love with me."

Startled by the request, Dr. Blake Di Angelo tapped his thumbs against the sleek surface of his mahogany desk, thinking that perhaps the petite blonde pacing across his Knoxville medical office had already gone mad.

"You'll have to repeat that, Darby." He leaned against his leather chair's backrest, eyeing her with more than a little curiosity. "Because I don't think I heard you right."

His business partner paused long enough to bestow a glance on the bluest eyes that side of the Mississippi. Eyes that were usually sparkling with laughter. Not today. Today, her fingers clenched around a card of some sort,

Dr. Darby Phillips' eyes were clouded with displeasure.

"You owe me." Her expression dared him to deny her claim. "Last weekend of the month. You're going with me to Alabama and you're going to pretend to be goo-goo-ga-ga, head-over-heels in love with me the entire time."

His brow arching at her determined expression, Blake grinned. God, she was bossy. He liked it. Had always liked Darby's assertiveness and self-assurance. From the time he'd met her four years ago, she'd been driven to be the best at everything she did.

"Why am I going to do this?" He couldn't resist teasing. Mostly because he knew how to push her buttons to have her going from zero to through the roof.

She started pacing again. "Because you owe me, and I'm collecting."

Blake's eyes traveled over her curvy little frame encased in a no-nonsense navy business suit, exposing shapely legs beneath her skirt hem. The shirt was tucked into a waist that his hands would probably fit around. Her breasts—well, he knew better than to let his thoughts go there. He valued their business relationship too much to acknowledge her as the desirable woman she so obviously was.

"And because of this." She tossed the embossed card onto his desk and shuddered. "Which I'd completely forgotten about."

She turned those big baby-blues on him again, stared with such beseeching that his insides shifted off axis enough to make his world wobble, to make him want to take her into his arms and promise he'd fix whatever had her so upset.

"How could I have forgotten that was this year? This month?" Panic brewing in the blue depths, her gaze bored into him. "I really don't need the headache of looking for a date who'll no doubt get the wrong idea by an invitation to something so personal. But I do need a man for that weekend." Taking a deep breath, she lifted her shoulders and took on the expression of a seasoned soldier, readying for battle. "Tag, you're it."

Blake picked up the card and studied the fancy maroon and gold embossing more closely. Armadillo Lake Ten-Year High School Reunion. "Don't they usually give folks more notice than two weeks for these kinds of things?"

Darby muttered something under her breath. "Usually."

"You could go without a date."

"Oh, no." Stray pale blonde tendrils loosened from her upswept hair danced at her almost violent headshake. "I'd rather not go than go dateless."

"Then don't go. Problem solved. No one says you have to go to your high school reunion."

Although he had meant to, he hadn't gone to his. Darby had been sick with the flu and he'd covered for her at the hospital instead. No big deal, since he'd moved so often he'd never gotten particularly attached to any of the numerous private prep schools he'd attended.

She let out an exasperated sound. "It's not that simple. Besides, you owe—"

"Yes, I know," he conceded. "I owe you for bailing me out last month, when it was my turn to be on call and I wanted to go out of town." A weekend that had ended in disaster when his then girlfriend had got wedding bells on her brain. He liked his life as it was and had no intention of marrying. For one reason or another, marriages didn't seem to work in his family. Besides, he was enjoying bachelorhood too much for that.

"So you have to go to your reunion." He dropped the invitation back onto his desk. "Why the 'in love' stuff?"

"Mandy Coulson." Darby's agitation tripled. Quadrupled.

Blake's curiosity grew accordingly. Even when under intense pressure, Darby rarely lost her cool. God, he'd loved to watch her work when they'd been in residency—still did. Calm, cool, in control. Today she was hot under the collar, sweating like any normal person, and not because of his teasing. No, although Blake had thought he knew better than anyone how to get a rise out of his pretty little partner, apparently this Mandy person and a high school reunion had him beat.

He didn't see what the big deal was, but he was intrigued as to why Darby did.

"And Mandy is…?" He stretched his hand out in question. "Who?"

"Every shy kid's worst nightmare." The words hissed from Darby's pursed lips like air escaping a rapidly deflating balloon.

Interesting. He had a hard time imagining the confident young woman he knew as shy. Ever.

This trip might prove to be educational.

He tossed the invitation on his desk and waggled his eyebrows mischievously. "Okay, *darling*, I'll be your boy toy."

Boy toy? As if. Darby rolled her eyes before meeting her partner's black-as-sin gaze. As attractive as she found Blake, the man went through women as if he were competing for a world record. That didn't mean she wasn't crazy about him—just that she knew better than to feed his oversized ego.

"Keep that up and you'll leave me no choice but to call Rodney," she threatened, knowing

Blake had never liked her recent attempt at dating. "If I pander to his ego a little—" a lot "—and tell him how rotten you are—" Rodney had been jealous of the "Italian Stallion", Rodney's label for Blake, not Darby's "—he's sure to go with me."

Although they'd only gone out for a couple of months, he was still calling her, trying to convince her they could make things work if only she'd have sex with him. Yeah, right. Not during this lifetime.

There was only one man she wanted to sleep with, and he had no clue that was how she felt.

"The hell you say," Blake growled. "He was the most suspicious man I've ever met— dropping by here all hours of the night." His strong jaw clenched, emphasizing the slight cleft in his chin. "What did he expect? To catch me with my pants down?"

For the first time since she'd stormed into his office her lips twitched. "Actually, that *is* what he expected."

And then some. She hadn't been able to

convince Rodney that Blake was nothing more than her business partner. Maybe because from the time they'd met she'd hoped Blake would see her for more than her brain and medical skills. After four years of his treating her much as one of her brothers did, she'd decided she didn't register on Blake's female radar. Just as well. None of the women he was interested in ever lasted long. Blake's love-life consisted of a revolving door and multiple women. She wanted him forever, not just for a few weekends.

So she'd waited, hoped, become more and more frustrated.

"He thought you were getting lucky." Since Rodney hadn't been getting lucky, he'd automatically assumed Blake, being the only other man in her life, must be. *Men.*

Blake waggled his brows again. "Well, you can't blame the guy for thinking I'd get lucky. I am irresistible."

"And so modest, too." She snorted at his mock-innocent expression. "Luck has nothing to do with how you get women."

His lips twitched. "Enlighten me. How *do* I get women?"

*Any way he wanted them.*

"With that jet-black hair and those dark-as-midnight eyes you don't have to get women, they get you." The laughter in those black eyes had her feet wanting to shift—or run for the closest exit. How had the conversation even taken this turn? Her face grew hot and her skin clammy.

"At least, women *try* to get you," she rushed on, hoping he didn't notice how uncomfortable talking about his love-life made her. "You're oblivious to most, yet they keep chasing you. So, like I said, you don't have to get women, they get you."

"And, like I said—" he rocked back in his chair and blatantly eyed her with amusement "—I'm irresistible."

Dimples cut into his cheeks, making her think perhaps he was right. Certainly she'd always wanted him. Then again, with so little experience when it came to men, how could she be expected *not* to fall for someone so skilled in the ways of the opposite sex?

Because if Blake's love-life was a revolving door, Darby's was a vault that had rusted shut long ago from lack of use.

"For example," he continued, "I was recently propositioned to spend the weekend with a beautiful woman." His black eyes twinkled. "I even get to pretend to be in love with her. How much luckier can a guy get?"

Picking up a spongy ball—a stress-reliever advertising a pharmaceutical firm—she tossed it at him. "I wouldn't count on getting lucky that particular weekend if I were you. You're not that irresistible."

At least not that she'd ever admit. But if she thought there was the slightest chance Blake could love her, she'd throw caution to the wind and make him notice she was a woman the weekend of the reunion.

He caught the stress ball with ease. "Come to think of it, my luck's never been *that* good. Just look at the last female who found me." He

cringed with revulsion and gave an exaggerated shudder.

Darby bit back a smile.

So the foolish physical therapist he'd been
dating on and off for a few months had thought
Blake was taking her out of town to pop the
question. Instead, the Yankees had been in
Atlanta, and a friend had given him Braves
tickets. Blake's proposal had consisted of, "Do
you want mustard or ketchup on your hot dog?"
When the game had ended, with no highlighted
proposal on the scoreboard, Kristi had issued an
ultimatum she'd regretted the moment Blake
had waved goodbye.

He interrupted her thoughts. "But you have to
admit I am better than Rodney."

True, but Rodney had been an okay boyfriend—a good start to her late-in-life attempt to
develop dating skills. Well, an okay boyfriend
except for his jealousy of Blake and how he'd
pushed for sex. After Blake had dumped Kristi in
Atlanta, Rodney's possessiveness had suffocated
Darby. He would view going to her high school

reunion as moving their relationship into another realm. A realm where she didn't want to go, as she had no intention of having sex with him. Ever.

Blake was right. He was the better choice in so many ways.

No one from her past would expect to see her with a man like Blake. With him at her side she could pretend she wasn't still the geeky girl who'd left Armadillo Lake with big dreams and stars in her eyes.

She picked up the invitation to return to Armadillo Lake, Alabama. Her hometown.

She had to go.

Had to prove Mandy Coulson wrong. Prove her entire class wrong. Prove to herself that she really was the confident young woman she looked at in the mirror each morning. She was, wasn't she?

Her hand clenched around the invitation Mandy had no doubt delayed in sending.

She'd go home with her head held high, with a gorgeous hunk attending to her every whim, and she'd show them all how wrong they were.

Or pretend to, at any rate.

And if along the way Blake discovered she was a girl behind her lab coat and high IQ— well, that would be icing on the cake, now, wouldn't it?

Blake stepped into Darby's office during the week of the reunion. "Can I get your opinion on Mr. Hill's leg?"

It was late Tuesday evening and Darby had already finished with her last patient for the day. She glanced up from the computer screen where she researched an unusual plethora of symptoms a patient had come in with that morning.

"Nathan Hill, from Strawberry Plains?"

"That's the one." He skimmed his fingers over the model of the heart on top of her bookshelf. It was a running joke that he had heart envy. Every time he came into her office he touched the plastic heart. Someday she'd give the darn thing to him.

"I just examined him," Blake continued, "but since you were the last one to see the ulcer on his lower extremity, I wanted your opinion on whether you think it's improved."

"Sure thing." She bookmarked her page on the web and followed him into the exam room.

"Hi, Mr. Hill." She washed her hands and slid on a pair of disposable gloves. "Dr. Di Angelo has asked me to take a look at the place on your leg since I'd checked you a week or so ago." She smiled at the thin gentleman, patted his wrinkled hand. "How do you think it looks? Better? Worse? Or about the same?"

"Better," the seventy-year-old said. Unfortunately, Mr. Hill would say his leg was doing better even if his toes were black. Very simply, the man wouldn't complain. He'd just smile his toothless smile and tell her how he was doing just fine.

Squatting to examine his leg, Darby winced at the oozing ulcer that encompassed a good portion of his shin.

"Have you been taking the antibiotics I prescribed?" she asked, concerned that he'd gotten worse rather than better. "The culture I did on the area says the one prescribed should clear the infection, but obviously the medicine isn't working."

"I got the prescription filled." He scratched his mostly bald head with a thickened yellow nail that curved over the tip of his arthritic finger. "Only took a few. Figured I'd wait and see if I really needed them."

What was he waiting for? His foot to fall off? For the bacteria to build resistance to the antibiotics since he'd taken just enough to tease the infection?

Darby shook her head. "I stressed the importance of taking the antibiotics because they are vital to this area healing." She looked to where Blake stood. He'd entered the room with her, had been ready to assist if she needed anything, but was confident enough to stand back and let her do her job. She liked that about Blake. He trusted her, found her competent. Turning her gaze back to her patient, she gave him her most serious look. "I'd like to admit you to the hospital, give IV antibiotics for a few days, and keep a close eye on your leg."

Not liking Darby's assessment, Mr. Hill turned to Blake for another opinion. "Doc?"

"Admitting you to the hospital is what I was thinking, too, but you kept insisting you were better. Since I hadn't seen the way the area originally looked, I gave you the benefit of doubt." Blake raised a brow at Mr. Hill, who had the grace to blush. "Obviously you over-exaggerated."

Darby removed her gloves and tossed them into the appropriate disposal bin. She wrapped her arm around the older man and gave him a hug. "Obviously."

"It's not that bad," he insisted, giving Darby's hand a pat. "Definitely not bad enough to go to the hospital."

"You know I try to listen to my patients, Mr. Hill, and to take earnest consideration of their desires, but your leg is serious enough to warrant a hospital admission." Stepping back slightly, she took his hand into hers. "If the infection doesn't clear you could lose your foot. Do you understand? That isn't something I take lightly. Neither should you."

That got the older man's attention. She hadn't been meaning to scare him, but his ulceration was a big deal, and truly could result in amputation in someone with his poor circulation and diabetes. She spoke with him a few more minutes while Blake wrote admission orders to give to the man's daughter, who was waiting in the reception area.

Blake stuck the orders inside an envelope. "You give these to the lady at the admission desk. She'll register you."

They saw him out and spoke with his daughter, letting her know what was going on and stressing that even if her father changed his mind about going to the hospital, he really did need to go. When she'd brought the car around they saw him into the passenger seat, then made their way back toward the office.

"Do you want me to look in on him this evening and do the admission history and the physical?" Blake held the front door open for her to enter ahead of him. "Technically, I was the one to see him today."

"If it's all the same, I'll do the H and P when I check on Evie Mayo."

"Is she any better?"

Darby shook her head. "Unfortunately no. Her liver enzymes are through the roof and I can't find a reason why. Her hepatic ultrasound and her CT scan were both essentially normal. Only fatty streaks showed."

"Hepatitis profile okay?"

"All normal."

"You want me to take a look at her? See if I can come up with anything?"

Darby shrugged. "If you'd like. Maybe I'm missing something."

"I doubt that," he assured her, lightly punching her shoulder in a move her older brothers had often done when she'd been growing up. How long had it been since she'd seen Jim, John, Jerry and Ralph? Too long, since she'd opted to work last Christmas instead of making the six-hour drive to Armadillo Lake. She'd meant to go, but after Blake's mother had canceled plans last-minute to come to Knoxville for the holidays Darby hadn't been able to bear the thought of him alone at Christmas.

"But it never hurts to have a fresh eye give a second opinion," he continued. "Speaking of second opinions, what do I need to pack for this weekend?"

Dread filled her stomach. Was she really going to subject Blake to her humiliating high school experiences?

Of course, she was. Because she wasn't that shy, geeky girl who'd rather have had her nose stuck in a book than in a fashion magazine. She was a successful doctor with a fabulous life.

Okay, so she didn't have a real boyfriend, and was bringing her business partner instead, but no one had to know that the scrumptious man with her wasn't madly in love with her.

Her gaze landed on Blake. He *was* scrumptious to look at—the classic tall, dark and handsome—and she was half in lust with him, so that had to count for something, right?

No one would accuse her of being a virgin when she had a virile man like Blake making googly eyes at her. Which should be enough to ease the bile burning her throat, yet wasn't.

Why wasn't she eagerly anticipating the chance to prove to Armadillo Lake just how wrong they'd been about her? Surely she wasn't still intimidated by her classmates? By Mandy?

No way.

Or maybe she *was* intimidated, because at times she wondered if they'd been right about her. After all, she was a twenty-eight-year-old virgin. By choice, but still a virgin.

Maybe her nervousness stemmed from the man before her. Had she really asked Blake to pretend to be in love with her? To spend the weekend with her, share a hotel room with her?

"Saturday afternoon is a picnic at the town park, so something casual for that. The reunion itself is being held at the Armadillo Lake Lodge's ballroom and will be dressy. Not tuxedo formal, but you'll need a suit." She raked her gaze over him, imagining him at the party.

He'd look good in a tux, but that would definitely be overkill. A tux would scream "trying too hard". She wanted their relationship to look real, not make-believe.

She wanted their relationship to be real, not make-believe.

She bit back a sigh. Their relationship *was* real. They had a great business relationship, were ideal partners. Anything beyond that would only make life complicated, because if she and Blake ever became involved that way she'd end up hurt and losing everything. But what if…?

"Picnic and dressy." Winking, he shot her with his finger. "Gotcha."

Fighting to look as if her mind wasn't racing in unwanted directions, she lifted her shoulders. "Wear that blue button-down you bought for the hospital Christmas party last year. I like how that looks on you."

His brow quirked. "Tell me, which part do you like?"

Darby winced. Had she really just said that she liked how his shirt fit him?

"The part that covers you up," she quipped, stepping into the back hallway leading to their private offices. No way would she admit to liking how the material emphasized his broad shoulders and narrow waist.

"Now, now," he chided, "that's not how you should be talking to the man you're madly in love with."

Certain her heart throbbed in her throat, despite knowing such a feat was physically impossible, Darby froze, rounded on him. "I'm not madly in love with you."

She might have feelings for Blake, but she didn't do love. At the young age of sweet sixteen she'd learned that love hurt way too much, and credited herself with being intelligent enough not to make the same mistake twice.

"Oh?" His brow lifted again, high enough that a lock of his inky hair hid the top of the arch. "Is this a one-sided love affair, then? I'm insane for you, but you're immune to my charms?" His lips twitched. "Or are you just using me for phenomenal sex?"

Trying not to think of phenomenal sex and Blake in the same context, Darby gulped. "You're crazy."

Perhaps she was crazy, too. Otherwise why would she have asked him to go to Armadillo Lake? Even forgetting how she'd deal with spending a weekend in a hotel room with him, he'd tease her mercilessly over the things he'd learn about the old Darby. She'd never live down the jokes, the puns.

"We really should get our story straight before this weekend." He took her elbow, led her into her office, pausing only long enough to caress the heart model as they passed by the shelf. "Maybe we should practice."

"Practice?" Darby's ears roared. Her heart thudded, pounding wildly against her ribcage and threatening to once again leap into her throat. Her gaze dropped to his lips and the desire to practice hit so hard she thought she might faint.

Then the most brilliant idea hit her. One in which she'd risk everything—but some risks were worth taking.

# CHAPTER TWO

"Do you even like the people you went to school with?" Blake stuck a French fry in his mouth. Although he usually ate healthily, French fries were his Achilles' heel. The hotter and saltier the better. Thanks to the hospital cafeteria ladies knowing his vice, they always put on a fresh batch just for him.

"Of course I like them," Darby insisted, but color rose in her cheeks. "I went to high school with them."

"Doesn't mean you like them." He stuck another fry in his mouth, assuring himself the five miles he ran each morning would clear out the excessive cholesterol. "I've never heard you mention anyone you went to school with."

"That doesn't mean I don't like them. I had some good friends back in school."

"So good that you're bringing a fake date to impress them?"

She didn't meet his eyes, took a sip of her water. "You should be flattered, since you get to be the impressive fake date."

"There is that," he mused, studying her, trying to get a feel for whatever it was she was hiding.

And Darby *was* hiding something.

He couldn't put his finger on what, but something had her buzzing about the prospect of returning to Armadillo Lake.

"Tell me about your hometown."

Her face pinched into a scowl. "Not much to tell."

Right.

"I'm going to your reunion this weekend. Don't you think I should know a little about your past?"

"Not really." Her nose curled, as if she'd taken a sniff of something vile. "We've known each other for what—four years? What you don't already know, you don't need to know."

"I disagree." What did he know about her past? Not much. Just that she'd grown up in a small town in Alabama, gone to medical school in Knoxville, on full scholarship, and had decided to stay in Tennessee after he'd jokingly suggested opening a practice together. Surprisingly, since he hadn't made up his mind on where he'd end up, when Darby had said yes, he'd known practicing with her was exactly what he wanted to do. Not once had he regretted that decision, and for the first time since his grandfather's death he had roots.

"Oh?" She might have meant the word to be nonchalant, but the slight squeak gave away her anxiety.

A good person might have let the subject go, not put her on the spot, but Blake had never claimed to be good. Not in that sense, at any rate.

He zeroed in on the one name she'd let slip on the day the invitation had arrived. "I want to know more about Mandy Coulson."

Darby sighed, rolling her eyes toward the

hospital cafeteria's ceiling. "You *would* want to know more about her, wouldn't you?"

He shrugged. "She's the only non-related person from your hometown I've ever heard you mention by name."

Her eyes flashed blue fire and her chin lifted. "Trey Nix."

Blake paused, fry midway to his mouth, dangling from his fingers. Trey Nix? "Who's he?"

Why did he instantly dislike him?

Face full-bloom pink, Darby pretended fascination with her chicken salad, raking her fork through the half-eaten entree. "No one."

Clearly she regretted having mentioned the name.

"No one?" He wasn't buying that. "Then why bring him up?"

"You insisted upon another name, and I knew you wouldn't quit until I gave you one."

"And Trey Nix—" what kind of name was Trey Nix, anyway? "—was the person who popped into your head?"

"It's just a name."

Uh-huh.

"Interesting."

Her gaze lifted to his. "What's so interesting?"

"That you mention a sworn enemy and then a guy." Pink blotches spread across her throat and Blake's suspicions rose. "Were you in a love triangle with Mandy and what's-his-name?"

"A *love triangle*?" She laughed. "You're crazy."

But the half-strangled way she said the words hinted that he'd hit the nail over the head.

"Besides I never said Mandy was my sworn enemy."

"No?" Good thing Darby had wanted to go into medicine and not acting. Not even the most gullible bloke would buy the bull she was attempting to feed him. Not liking how his fries weighed heavily in his stomach, he waited until her gaze met his. "Who was she?"

Better still, who was Trey Nix, and what had he meant to Darby?

Setting her fork next to her plate, she arranged the utensil on the tray. "For the first fifteen years of my life Mandy was my best friend."

Best friend? Now, there was a twist Blake hadn't seen coming.

The cafeteria wasn't crowded, or particularly noisy, but he had to strain to hear her next words.

"But that was before."

"Before what?"

She shook her head. "Let's change the subject. I've had enough of the past for one night, and no amount of poking or prodding from you is going to get me to say more, so let it go."

She dug into her salad with gusto. She'd been playing with her food all evening. He doubted she was even hungry. But apparently she didn't want to talk about Mandy and was sending a loud message for him to back off.

Her tone had switched to Darby bossy. The tone she used when he'd pushed as far as she would allow him to push.

Fine—he'd let the topic of Mandy go. For now.

"At least tell me what you expect of me this weekend."

She paused mid-bite. Startled eyes lifted to his. "What do you mean? I told you what I expected. Just pretend you're madly in love with me—as if I'm the greatest thing that's ever happened to you and you can't live without me."

"Okay," he said slowly, taking measure of the panic in her eyes and wondering at his own rising panic at her words. "I can do that."

In many ways, meeting Darby *was* the best thing to ever happen to him.

"How long have we been dating?"

She blinked at him, as if he'd spoken in an alien tongue. "Pardon?"

"There are things inquiring minds will want to know. Questions that are usually asked when a person sees someone they haven't seen in a while." He gave her a pointed look. "How long have we been dating?"

"The simpler we make this, the better." Glancing down at her plate, Darby stared at her food. "We'll say we've known each other for years, but only recently became romantically involved. Let's stick to the truth as much as possible."

Why was she so nervous? Because she was going to see the man from her past she'd mentioned? What did it matter to Blake? He should be happy if she reconnected with some long-lost love.

*Was* Nix a long-lost love?

Blake's fries threatened to stage an uprising. "The truth works for me."

"Except that you're in love with me," she pointed out.

His irrational reaction to the idea of Darby having a long-lost love irritated Blake. "I got that."

Her gaze dropping to her plate, she nodded. "I just wanted to be clear."

"As crystal."

Her cellphone rang. She pulled out the phone and looked at the number. Grimacing, she shoved the phone into her pocket.

"Who was that?"

"Rodney."

Her ex? Why was he calling? "You didn't change your mind about getting back with him?"

He hoped not. Really hoped not.

He didn't like the idea of Darby with Rodney. She was way too good for the guy. Plus, crazy as it was, he wanted to go with her this weekend, wanted to meet Mandy. And maybe even Trey Nix, just so he could figure out what Darby's relationship had been with the man—although he had a pretty good idea.

An idea he didn't like any better than the idea of Rodney.

"No," she sighed, looking tired, as if this trip home weighed heavily upon her mind.

He knew she hadn't gone home last Christmas, but she had made the trip when her niece was born. During the four years he'd known her she'd gone home a few times a year, but never for more than a night.

"Part of me wonders if I should beg him to take me back rather than bring you to my hometown."

No, she shouldn't bring Rodney with her. Blake wanted to meet her family, see where she'd grown up, figure out what it was about her hometown that made a woman he admired for her confidence so unsure of herself.

Darby was his partner and she needed his help. More than she even realized. Whatever her issues were with her hometown, he'd help her. He owed her that for keeping him on task throughout his residency and the beginning of his medical career.

"I can behave myself. Even in a place named Armadillo Lake." He chuckled, letting the name roll off his tongue. "Sounds like a fun place to grow up. Is there really a lake?"

"Yes."

"And armadillos?"

"Yes."

"Your school team were the Armadillos?"

She gritted her teeth. "Yes."

"Let me guess—your school mascot was a giant armadillo?"

Gaze lowered to her plate, Darby nodded.

"Bet that went over great at football games." He chuckled. "An armadillo."

Darby had grown still. She looked as if she were praying he wouldn't put two and two together. Where Darby was concerned Blake always put two and two together. He grinned.

"You were the mascot, weren't you?"

* * *

The next morning Darby had barely climbed out of her car before Blake fell into step beside her in the clinic's employee parking lot. "I checked on Mr. Hill this morning. He's insisting on going home, and he's only been there one night."

She ignored him, just as she'd been ignoring him since he'd burst out laughing at her admission she'd once worn an armadillo suit to all major school sport events.

Not a cute little armadillo suit that showed off her legs—if such a suit even existed. No, she'd been in a full-bodied, hot-as-Hades, head-to-toe vinyl Armadillo suit that looked like something straight off a cheap Godzilla movie. And all to impress a guy—to prove that she was more than a brainy girl, that she had a sense of humor and could be fun. What had she been thinking?

"He's giving the nurses a hard time." With his usual persistence, Blake continued, following her down the clinic's hallway toward their offices. "The night nurse said he pulled out his IV line. She put the line back in, and threatened to strap his hands to the bedrails if he pulls it out again."

Darby already knew all this. She'd visited Mr. Hill, too. Blake had beaten her to the hospital, thanks to her sleeping late, but she had checked on her two patients this morning.

No wonder she'd overslept. Most of the night she'd lain in bed having nightmares about the upcoming weekend. Nightmares in which she'd shown up at the reunion not decked out to the nines as planned, in the new killer dress she'd bought, but wearing that awful armadillo suit. Trey hadn't been the one laughing at her. Blake had been the one shaking his head, pointing his finger, not understanding her desire to fit in. Not understanding how she desperately wanted him to notice that she was alive. The truth, she'd realized, was that this weekend was more about *him* than her class reunion.

She'd awakened in a cold sweat, certain she'd made a grave miscalculation—that thinking she could make Blake notice her as a woman was as foolish as wearing that armadillo suit had been.

Despite having sent in her RSVP, she didn't have to go. Most likely no one would even notice if she was there or not.

No, that wasn't true.

Mandy would know. Wasn't that why she'd sent Darby's invitation late?

If she didn't go, she was saying that she was okay with her and Blake's relationship never being more than what it was. And, although what they had was wonderful, Darby wanted more.

She was going.

Not only was she going, but she was going to have fun.

And in the process of making Blake notice her she'd make Trey eat his heart out because he'd chosen the head cheerleader over the geeky, too-smart-to-be-understood school mascot. *What had he been thinking?*

She'd risen beyond her high school experiences and was a desirable woman who held the power over her life. Wasn't that what her wannabe-shrink roommate during her first four years at university had said—making Darby repeat the phrase while looking in the mirror each morning, insisting Darby go for formal self-confidence-boosting therapy?

She was in charge of her life. Dr. Darby Phillips, a woman worthy of respect and admiration. A woman who'd come a long way from wearing a dumpy armadillo suit and longing for a man she couldn't have.

Her gaze fell on the man keeping stride next to her.

Well, no one could accuse her classy navy pants and cream-colored blouse of looking like a scaly animal, at any rate.

"Ah, come on, Dilly, surely you aren't still mad at me?"

*Why had she told him the mascot's name?*

Blake being Blake, of *course* he'd tease her, call her by that name. She spun to where he'd followed her into her office.

Knocking his hand away from her plastic heart model, she straightened to her full five feet three inches and poked his thick chest. "Don't you ever make fun of my having been an armadillo again—do you hear?"

His eyes widened slightly at her outburst, but a smile curved his full lips. "Ah, Darby, come on. I'm sure you were a cute armadillo."

She glared. He was supposed to be groveling, shaking in fear, apologizing, not still laughing.

"Too bad I didn't go to your school." He tweaked her chin, his fingers sending shivers over her flesh. "I'd like to have seen you in that costume. Maybe you could wear it for me this weekend? I promise to show my school spirit."

Couldn't he be serious? Or at least pretend as if he felt threatened? Of course he couldn't. Blake was one of those annoying perpetually positive folks. As much as that did annoy her at times like these, his disposition was also one of the things she liked most about him. One of the things that had always drawn her to him.

He made her laugh. Had from the moment they'd met. She'd been so serious, so determined never to let a man make a fool of her again, so focused on getting her medical degree, she'd forgotten how to laugh until she and Blake had been assigned an emergency room rotation together. She might have been up to her eyeballs in work, but one wink from Blake could re-energize her sleep-deprived body and have her smiling from the inside out.

No one had ever been able to make her feel good the way he could.

Fighting to hang on to her angry bravado, she rolled her eyes. "The only costume you need to see me in is a white lab coat." She forced her brows into a scowl. "Isn't it time for us to get started seeing patients?"

He sighed with exaggerated effort. "You're in a foul mood this morning, Dilly."

She pursed her lips, crossed her arms and glared up at him. Way up. Why had she worn flats? "No more armadillo jokes."

She refused to back down. She didn't want Blake seeing her in the same light Trey had. After a moment of their facing off—her feigning anger, him grinning—he nodded.

"Fine, no more school mascot jokes." He put his fingers up in a Scout's Honor symbol. "If I get the urge to tease you, I'll just *dill* with it."

She looked heavenward. "This isn't funny."

He lifted one shoulder in a half-shrug. "From where I'm standing, it's pretty funny."

"Because you weren't the one wearing that horrible suit."

Perhaps she'd let too much of her past pain bleed through, because Blake stared at her a little too closely.

"Last I heard, folks aren't forced to be school mascots," he pointed out. "They volunteer for the job."

"Well, Mr. Know-it-all, sometimes there are extenuating circumstances that cause a girl to wear ugly suits and play a fool."

"What extenuating circumstances?" His dark eyes saw too much, and Darby fought from shifting her weight.

"It's complicated." Complicated? Yet another word for humiliating herself in an effort to get Trey's attention

Looking way too serious, Blake crossed his arms in a similar stance to her own. "I've got time."

There were some things that shouldn't be repeated. Her high school blunders were just a few of them. She glanced at her watch. "I don't. I need to see my morning patients. Bye."

She grabbed her stethoscope and rushed from the office. Without turning to check, she could feel his gaze burning into her, could feel the heat scorching her cheeks.

She also sensed his amusement. His curiosity.

"See you later, Dilly," he called from behind her, no doubt brushing his fingers over her heart model.

What had she been thinking when she'd told him about that wretched costume? About her nickname? Next thing she knew she'd tell him she'd been voted most likely to die a virgin and had yet to do anything to prove her classmates wrong. For a woman who prided herself on her intelligence, she sure was making a lot of stupid choices.

But there came a time when a woman had to either don an armadillo suit—or invite a man to spend a weekend in a hotel with her in hopes of being noticed or accept not registering on his radar.

As insane as her frustration was, Darby was tired of not making a bleep on Blake's radar.

She wanted his radar bleeping. For her.

Which just went to prove how little intelligence she really had.

Bleeping on Blake's radar would likely ruin everything she held dear, so why was she bleep, bleep, bleeping in her heart?

The closer Darby and Blake got to Armadillo Lake on Friday afternoon, the more Darby's stomach churned.

What was wrong with her?

She should be looking forward to the opportunity to return home and show her old schoolmates they'd been wrong about her on most accounts. And she should be excited at the prospect of maybe making Blake see her as a desirable woman…

After all, hadn't that been the idea behind her last-minute shopping trip to her favorite lingerie shop? She should be a lot of things, but she suspected if Blake wasn't the one behind the wheel she'd turn the SUV around and head back to Tennessee pronto. For so many reasons—not the least of which was that she was afraid of what the weekend might do to her and Blake's relationship.

But if she wanted more than what she had— and she did—she had to shake things up. Sleeping in the same bed should do that—had he even considered their sleeping arrangements when she'd invited him?

Darby stole a glance toward him and fought a very feminine sigh of appreciation. God, he was breathtaking. And, for the weekend, he was all hers.

"You've barely spoken the last thirty miles of our drive."

"You've talked enough for the both of us," she pointed out.

He had. Blake could carry on a conversation with a stump. His gift of the gab was a trait she envied. Although she'd taken classes to help her overcome her shyness, she'd been introverted for the earlier years of her life. She hadn't wanted to be shy, but when you preferred to have your nose stuck in a book than to drive into Pea Ridge to cruise the shopping mall— well, popularity wasn't your middle name.

"Didn't your mom tell you not to do that? Your face might get stuck like that."

Designer aviator glasses protected Blake's eyes from the blazing sunshine brightening their drive. If the manufacturer could hire him to model those shades, they'd sell billions. He made them look that good.

"Like what?" she asked, thinking life was unfair if one man could have been blessed with so many talents. Looks, intelligence, wit. Yet, Blake wasn't one of those men who walked around thinking he was a million bucks. Despite his teasing about his many charms, he was one of the most genuine persons she knew. Actually, he was *the* most genuine person she knew. What you saw was what you got.

She liked what she saw way too much.

"Like we just drove past another chicken barn with the windows down."

Darby bit the inside of her lip to keep from smiling. Not long after they'd crossed the Alabama state line Blake had rolled down the windows to experience some fresh country air. He'd gotten fresh country air, all right.

"Most likely we did pass another one."

This time it was his face that wrinkled—him who looked like he might need to pull the SUV over.

"I'll never eat chicken again."

Darby laughed out loud. "There are chicken barns in Tennessee. So don't tell me you'd never experienced a chicken barn up close and personal before."

"Apparently I'm still a city boy at heart," he admitted unashamedly. "From the car is as up close and personal as I want to get to a barn of any type. Especially one as foul as what we smelt earlier."

"Foul?" Shaking her head at his double entendre, Darby laughed again. Just as well she wasn't planning to take him with her when she dropped in on her folks tonight.

Her stomach jerked again. No doubt her brothers and their wives would start pushing for her to move home. They always did. Her family hadn't been able to understand why she'd been so driven to leave Armadillo Lake, to get her degree and make something of herself, to see the world. They especially hadn't understood when her plans to join a traveling medical program had taken a one-eighty turn and she'd stayed in Knoxville.

Then again, they'd never met Blake.

"What were you thinking about that made you scowl?"

She should have known he wouldn't let her change the subject. He rarely did.

"About the reunion."

He glanced away from the road just long

enough for her gaze to meet the mirrored lenses that hid his eyes. He shook his head in confusion. "Most people look forward to high school reunions, to catching up with their old classmates, seeing who married who, who has the most kids, who gained forty pounds, who still has their hair."

"Yeah, well." She turned to stare out the window at the growing all too familiar landscape, her belly lurching. "I'm not most people, City Boy."

"That you're not." He chuckled, then surprised her by reaching across the gap between their seats and taking her hand into his.

Clasping their fingers together, he squeezed.

Her belly gave another jolt, a much larger one than before, and she faced him.

"No worries, Darby. Whatever it is that has you wound so tightly about this weekend, everything is going to be fine. You're going to dazzle all your old classmates with your intelligence, success, beauty, and especially with your impressive date." Smiling, he briefly dipped his head, glancing at her from above the rim of his shades. His black eyes bored into her. "I promise."

The warmth emanating from Blake's hand to hers almost made her believe everything would be all right concerning the reunion—that every fantasy she'd ever had of returning to Armadillo Lake and making everyone eat armadillo… er…crow, would come true.

Regarding the way every single cell in her body surged to life at how his hand still held hers, at how much she liked his hand holding hers, at how many hopes she had pinned to their spending the weekend together—well, that was another matter altogether.

# CHAPTER THREE

FOR the dozenth time since they'd arrived at the Armadillo Lake Lodge, Darby stared at the queen-sized bed monopolizing the standard hotel room.

"Forget it," Blake warned, stepping next to her. His hands rested on his lean hips as he stared at the bed, too. "I'm not sleeping in a chair."

He thought she wanted him out of the bed? What would he say if she admitted to having been imagining the two of them there? To wondering what it would be like to spend the entire weekend in bed with him? Laughing, playing…something more…?

He'd probably laugh and tell her to be serious.

She sighed, shaking the bottle of fruity disinfectant she'd sprayed onto the top of the gaudy brown and orange comforter that likely had been in use since the lodge had first opened.

"I didn't say you had to sleep in a chair."

If they didn't share the bed, news would spread like wildfire. *This was Armadillo Lake.* Everyone knew everyone's business. After cleaning the room, Gertrude Johnson would no doubt spill the juicy tidbit to anyone who'd listen. The Johnsons had run the only hotel within a thirty-mile radius for as long as Darby could remember. If not for the tearoom that served as the town's only "nice" restaurant, and the large ballroom that hosted all major town events, the place would likely have gone out of business years ago. Armadillo Lake didn't attract many tourists.

Just unsuspecting women returning for their high school reunion while trying to convince the man of her dreams that she was the woman of his dreams. No biggie.

She turned to look at him. Despite their six-hour drive, he looked crisp. Not a wrinkle on the gorgeous man's khaki shorts that fell to just above his knees, nor on his expensive polo shirt. Just once she'd like to see him rumpled.

Her gaze shot back to the bed.

Okay, so she wanted to rumple him and rumple him thoroughly. More than once. A girl could dream, couldn't she?

She swallowed.

She had to quit this fantasy stuff. Blake was here to help her. If their near proximity helped him see her as a female, then so be it—but she didn't plan to throw herself at him. Either Blake wanted a relationship with her or he didn't.

Her gaze fell on the bed again.

"The bed's plenty big for the both of us. We'll share." She narrowed her eyes to what she hoped were menacing slits. "You stay on your side, and I'll stay on mine."

"Dibs on the top side."

"Fine, you can have that top side, and I'll take this top side." She pointed to the side of the bed closest to the bathroom for herself.

"That wasn't exactly what I meant." He laughed, watching her lift the comforter and spray disinfectant between the sheets and on the underside of the comforter. "You're the only person I know who disinfects hotel room beds."

Darby shrugged. She wasn't exactly a germ-a-phobe. But she'd seen one too many television specials about what crawled around in hotel room beds not to come prepared, and she always brought her own pillow.

"Here." She tossed the spray bottle to him. "You're a big boy. Disinfect your own side."

Catching the bottle, he grinned. She turned to unpacking her clothes. Holding her breath, she pulled a black lacy number from her suitcase and dropped it into the drawer she'd also disinfected.

She glanced up in time to see Blake's gaze following her movements as she dropped another pair of tiny panties into the drawer.

His feet shifted. He swallowed. He tugged on the collar of his polo shirt.

When his gaze met hers, Darby had no doubts.

If this weekend accomplished nothing else, Blake had just realized she was a woman.

A woman who had a predilection for fancy undergarments.

In that moment, Blake wanted her.

She'd wanted him always.

Now what? Could her fantasies become realities, or would her hopes only lead to disaster?

Still fighting his reaction to the skimpy silk scraps Darby had pulled from her suitcase, Blake hung his clothes in the hotel room's tiny closet.

All these years he'd never known she had a penchant for sexy lingerie.

But why would he have known? They didn't have that type of relationship. Not one where they discussed boxers or briefs, granny whites or spidery webs of black silk. They were business partners—and he'd be a wise man to remember that instead of wondering how that tangled lace would look hugging her bottom.

The sound of something falling to the bathroom floor was followed by Darby mumbling something he couldn't make out through the closed door.

Pausing at the closet, he eyed his suit, hanging side-by-side next to Darby's brilliant blue dress. He reached out, ran his fingertips over the soft material of her dress.

Maybe he should pretend to sleep in the chair.

Pretend because even if the curved wooden chair that was designed more for looks than comfort was the most comfortable chair in the world there was no way he'd rest with Darby sleeping in the same room.

He hadn't thought doing this favor would be a big deal, but he'd never spent the weekend in a hotel with a beautiful woman he wasn't having sex with.

He sure hadn't ever slept in a bed with a woman he wasn't having sex with.

Especially when he wanted to be having sex with that woman.

But sex with Darby could never be just sex.

She was his business partner, his friend, someone he cared about.

All reasons why sex wasn't a good idea.

As much as he wanted to see Darby in those

tiny bits of silk, sex between them would ruin everything. Darby didn't do casual sex, and Blake didn't do anything but.

The bathroom door opened. Blake faced the woman he'd just been imagining in her underwear. Again. Trapped steam from her recent shower kissed his skin—or maybe that was sweat from his thoughts of what she had on underneath her clothes. She'd changed into a pair of white shorts that showed off her toned legs and a trendy top that showcased her full breasts and made her waist look tiny. Dampness clung to the hair at the base of her neck. The rest of her blonde hair was clipped by a toothed hairpiece that could double as a torture device.

"I'll be back in a few hours." Her eyes didn't meet his. "Don't wait up."

*Which of those silk numbers did she wear beneath her clothes?*

He swallowed, trying to dislodge the brick stuck in his throat. *Granny panties, Blake. She's wearing big, ugly granny panties. Just keep telling yourself that and eventually you'll forget what you saw, what you want to see wrapped around Darby's curvy body.*

"Blake?" Her forehead wrinkled with concern. "You okay?"

Okay? No, he wasn't okay. His imagination was working overtime. What she'd said registered in his lingerie intoxicated mind.

"If you're going out, I'm going with you." Wherever she was going, she wasn't leaving him in the hotel room. With her underwear and his over-active imagination. Hell, no.

"No." Her tone held full Darby bossiness. "You're not."

"If you think I'm sitting in a hotel room alone while you go out, think again." He closed the closet door, for once not appreciating her bossy attitude. "Where are you going anyway?"

"To my parents', and you're not going. End of discussion."

Her parents? Of course. Darby's family lived here. Just because his mother made moving house a hobby that didn't mean normal families changed addresses on an annual rotation. Why hadn't he considered that she'd want to visit while in Armadillo Lake?

"I'm coming with you," he said matter-of-factly, knowing he'd win this argument, "and you should be grateful."

Bingo. She lifted confused eyes to his. "Huh?"

He gave a smug smile. "How will it look if the man who is madly in love with you doesn't go to meet your parents? Tsk, tsk, Darby," he scolded, crossing his arms. "You're the one who said you wanted this to appear real. Twiddling my thumbs in our hotel room while you visit with the family doesn't work."

He watched the unhappy realization that he was right wash over her heart-shaped face, watched as she searched for a feasible argument, summarily dismissing each one.

"I don't want you to go." She dropped onto the bed in an unladylike flounce that had visions of skimpy underwear flashing in his brain again. "My parents don't know you're with me. But they do know I'm here." Her voice had taken on an unfamiliar whiny tone. "I have to go, but you can't go with me."

"Did you plan to hide me away in the hotel while you snuck in the obligatory visit with the family?" The guilt on her face said that was exactly what she'd intended. "I'm an easy-going guy, Darby, you know that. But I'm not doing room service while you go to your parents." He frowned. "We've been partners for almost a year and I've never met your family. Why is that?"

She'd met his mother on the rare occasions Cecelia had dropped by Knoxville for a visit. But he hadn't met a single person from Darby's pre-Knoxville life. Not even at the grand opening of their clinic.

"Fine. You can come." She stood, eyed him as if she'd rather kiss a sewer rat than introduce him to her family. "But just remember you insisted upon going and that I was going to spare you the drama." Then her eyes took on a delighted spark. "Oh, and by the way, City Boy, there are chicken barns. Four of them. Hope you're real hungry for some of my momma's chicken and dumplings. Mmm, *chicken*."

Darby winced. No, her mother *hadn't* really just pulled up her shirt to ask Blake's opinion on the "bug bites" on her abdomen. Not at the dining room table. Not with the entire family present. Not while they were eating dinner.

Yep, Nellie Phillips had.

To his credit, Blake was taking her family—all twenty-two of them present and accounted for, and sitting at various places throughout the farmhouse—in his stride. Actually, he seemed amused by the chaos that was a permanent fixture at the Phillips home.

Standing there with her floral print shirt pulled up, her mother revealed a tiny sliver of thick white cotton and a wide expanse of pale white skin, marred only by the bright red vesicles clustered over her lower ribcage and wrapping around her trunk on her left side.

Concern replacing her mortification, Darby squinted at the "bug bites". "Are you sure something bit you?"

Blake examined the rash. "Looks more like Herpes Zoster."

Darby agreed. Those angry clusters were isolated to a single dermatome, and hadn't been caused by an insect.

"Herpes Zoster? Is that serious?" one of her brothers asked, leaning toward his mother for a closer look. "See, Mom, I told you to let me drive you into Pea Ridge to be checked."

Nellie gave Jim a silencing look. "Don't be silly. Herpes Zoster is a fancy term for shingles."

"Shingles?" Darby's dad spoke up from where he sat in his honored spot at the head of the table. He lowered his glass of iced tea and scratched his graying head. "Earl Johnson from down the road—you remember him, Darby? You used to clean house for him? He had shingles early in the spring. Had me kill my rooster for him."

Knowing Blake didn't want to hear about old wives' tale remedies for certain ailments, Darby scooted her chair closer to the table and reached for the bowl of fried potatoes. "Mom, how long have you had the rash? Are you taking anything to help dry it up?"

"Tell Darby about those spells you've been having."

Darby's gaze cut from her mother to her oldest brother and back again. "What spells?"

Her mother waved her hand. "No big deal. Just a few twinges of pain. I thought from the bug bites."

Concern sparked in Darby's chest. "What kind of pain? Haven't you been feeling well?"

"I'm fine. Fit as a fiddle." Darby's mother didn't meet her eyes, but instead passed a bowl full of greens to Blake. "I remember my mother having shingles. She had a lot of pain even after the rash disappeared, complained with her side hurting for months."

"Pain is normal with shingles." Blake accepted the bowl, staring at the contents with speculative eyes. He tentatively dipped out a small spoonful. "You should schedule an appointment with your doctor to get on an antiviral and some pain medication."

"I don't like pills. Never have." Nellie smiled at Blake. "I'm like my mother that way."

Darby's niece came running into the kitchen, squealing that her brother had spilled his juice. Rosy jumped up to check on the spill, but Nellie placed her hand on her daughter-in-law's arm. "Let me."

Darby followed her mother into the living room and helped clean the juice puddle.

Watching her mother, Darby noticed the dark circles beneath her eyes. Dark circles she hadn't really noticed—probably because she'd been so distracted with worrying about Blake and his reaction to her family, worrying about her family's reaction to Blake. She also noticed the fatigue plaguing her mother's face, the deepening wrinkles, the slight tremble to her hand when she wiped the towel across the floor.

Her mother had shingles. Not the end of the world, but how long had she been suffering, ignoring the pain? Why hadn't she let Jim drive her to Pea Ridge to be checked? Why hadn't she mentioned the rash to Darby when they'd talked on the phone earlier in the week? Even if her mother didn't understand why she'd become a doctor, why she'd had to get away from Armadillo Lake, she knew she was a darn good one.

When they'd wiped up the last of the juice from the scuffed hardwood floor, Darby met her mother's gaze and felt as if she was five years old.

"Mom," she began, before they stepped back into the kitchen, "you didn't have to ask Blake about your rash. I would have checked it for you."

"Nonsense." Re-entering the kitchen, her mother waved her hand. "He's a *real* doctor." She shot an admiring glance toward where Blake sat talking with Darby's father. "No sense in you having to worry yourself over some little rash."

A real doctor. What was she? A pretend one?

Darby sighed.

Might as well be, since she was faking everything else this weekend.

Blake didn't have to be a rocket scientist to see that Darby was irritated with most of her family.

As the youngest of five children, and the only girl, her family treated her as if she were incapable of doing anything for herself. At each point Darby attempted to do something, even if it was only to refill her glass of tea, someone jumped in and did the task for her. Couldn't they see what a talented young woman she'd grown into? How much their attitude annoyed her?

Another part of him envied her the camaraderie, the loudness, the interactions that came with having a large family who so obviously adored her.

As a little boy he'd heard his grandfather talk about huge family gatherings back in Malta, but only Vic Di Angelo had come to the States to make his fortune. He'd met a lovely young New Yorker who'd died giving birth to their only child—Blake's mother. Victoria Di Angelo had gotten pregnant while a teenager and, although she'd married numerous times, she had never had more children, leaving Blake an only child. Since his grandfather's death family dinners had consisted of Blake and his mother in a nice restaurant in whatever city she currently lived in, making small talk while sipping on wine and pretending they had something in common other than memories of the gruff old man they'd both loved.

"More banana pudding, Dr. Di Angelo?" asked one of Darby's sisters-in-law. He couldn't recall which one of her brothers the tall redhead was married to, but she was obviously the mother of the three red-headed kids who ran in and out of the dining room every so often.

He was a tad jealous of the freedom the Phillips kids enjoyed. How exciting growing up in a place like this must be when compared to the fancy downtown apartments and condos he'd always lived in.

"Call me Blake—and no thanks on the pudding." He patted his flat stomach, thinking perhaps French fries had been knocked down a notch from the top of his food chain. "Wish I could, but I'm stuffed."

"Did he just say he's buff?" Another sister-in-law, giggled from across the table, fanning her face.

Blake grinned. Yeah, he liked Darby's family. A lot.

"I'd second that," another said, cradling her three-month-old daughter in her arms so she could nurse her.

When at the last minute she threw a baby blanket over her shoulder and soon-to-be-exposed breast, Blake felt Darby's relief much louder than he heard the soft sigh. Hoping to reassure her, he caught her eye, winked.

"I'm sorry," she whispered, leaning close to his ear.

Her warm breath tickled his ear, goosebumping his flesh, hyper-driving his heart rate.

"What for?" he asked, wondering if she'd apologized for making him so aware of her, for the fact that despite the table still being laden with delicious food all he could smell was her delicate floral scent. Or the fact that every time he looked at her he wanted to peel away her clothes to see what she wore beneath. And then he wanted to peel those away, too.

"For making you eat chicken, of course," she teased, but he read the truth in her eyes. Her worries centered around her assumption that he was enduring her family for her and was barely able to do so.

He would endure any unpleasantness for Darby—after all, they were business partners. But he was enjoying her family.

Well, except for the way her brothers kept glaring and asking leading questions about his intentions regarding their little sister.

That he could have lived without.

Then again, he'd never had a sister. If he had, he'd have been just as tough on any guy she brought home. Actually, knowing what he usually did with women, he'd have been tougher. If they knew what he wanted to do to Darby, her brothers should take him out behind one of those long barns.

"I think it's so romantic, you two working together and falling in love," the redheaded sister-in-law sighed dreamily, pulling a carrot-topped toddler into her lap.

"We worked together at the Co-Op during high school. I don't hear you calling *that* romantic," her husband pointed out, reminding Blake which brother she belonged with. Best as Blake could recall, Jim was Darby's oldest brother, and the only one to share his sister's deep blue eyes.

"'Cause folks fall in love down at the Co-Op all the time. I think it's the hormones they put in the feed. You just don't hear about two doctors falling in love." She sighed again, accepting wet kisses from the little boy who had his palms smashed against her cheeks. She laughed at her son's antics, then said to no one in particular, "It's like something you'd see on television."

"What she means," explained the brunette sister-in-law nursing her baby, "is that Armadillo Lake doesn't have a doctor, much less two. That's why they haven't heard of doctors falling in love except on T.V."

Blake blinked. "Armadillo Lake doesn't have a doctor?"

"Closest one is in Pea Ridge, a clear thirty miles away. That's the closest hospital, too." She gestured to the blanket covering her nursing baby. "I thought I was going to have to deliver this one here in the calfing barn."

The calfing barn? Did he really want to know? He turned to Darby, who conspicuously stared at her empty plate.

"I'm surprised you didn't set up a clinic here."

A wince crinkled Darby's forehead.

"We all hoped she'd settle down near Armadillo Lake—the actual lake and not just in town. She always loved that old plantation house down there," another sister-in-law explained. "Course that was before the mess with Trey."

Although she'd been sitting quietly, toying with her shirt hem, Darby's head shot up. She made a slashing motion across her throat to the pretty brunette who was ignoring her.

"He's single again, you know. That girl from up near Gadsden and him got divorced last fall," another added. "He moved back earlier this year and opened a plumbing repair shop. Business has been real good, I hear. He bought the old Jenson farm and is considered quite the catch."

"What mess?" Blake asked, wondering why a knot had formed in his stomach at the news Trey Nix was single and "quite the catch". Wondering why Darby's family waved Trey in front of Darby like a carrot. Was she supposed to be lured home?

She *had* a home. In Knoxville. With him.

"When Trey broke her heart, of course. High school quarterbacks are notorious for stealing girls' hearts around these parts." The brunette looked at her husband, who grinned back at her. Obviously Darby's youngest brother had been a quarterback who'd stolen *her* heart.

"Hello? I'm sitting right here," Darby reminded them, clanging her silverware against her plate. "Blake does not want to hear about Trey."

Actually, he did. But he took pity on the desperation in her eyes, knowing that before the weekend was over he'd learn what had transpired between his lovely partner and her high school quarterback.

But for now he'd play his role.

"Darby's right. I don't want to hear about men from her past, because they don't matter." He took her hand in his, laced their fingers for all to see. "She's mine now, and I plan to keep her."

Darby's mother beamed. A collective sigh came from the sisters-in-law. Her brothers exchanged looks. Her father shrugged.

Blake smothered a grin. He liked Darby's family. All of them. Why hadn't she introduced them in the past?

Next to him, she audibly caught her breath, and her eyes flashed with question. "Are you sure you don't want more dessert?"

He winked, letting her know he had this under control. She could thank him later for rescuing her from conversations about old heartbreaks.

Turning to Darby's mother, he flashed his most brilliant smile. "What I'd really like is to see Darby's baby photos. Got any you'd just love to show me?"

\* \* \*

Darby tried to ignore the fact that Blake's arm was around her, his hand pressing possessively into her lower back. She tried to ignore the fact that her sisters-in-law kept smiling at each other, that her brothers kept sizing Blake up, not quite sure what to make of him, that her parents were falling over themselves in hopes that he would save their baby girl from the follies of her youth by choosing medicine over marriage and children.

She was failing miserably, of course, and couldn't ignore any of those things, much less all of them.

No wonder. She and Blake sat squished next to each other on the same sofa she'd sat on when she'd still worn diapers. Her mother was on the opposite side of Blake, flipping through a family photo album and ecstatically pointing out various embarrassing pictures from Darby's youth.

She shook her head as Blake enthused over shot after shot—especially her "Dilly" photos.

Had he really asked to see her baby pictures? Had her family really not had an *aha!* moment and seen that this couldn't possibly be real? What man asked to see a woman's baby photos?

"The boys just hauled her with them wherever they went. She drove the tractor, helped haul hay—whatever they were doing, she was right in the middle. It's no wonder she was such a tomboy."

Dimples dug into Blake's cheeks, his eyes dancing with interest when he glanced toward Darby. "You were a tomboy?"

She shrugged. "For a while."

"Then she discovered books, and would hide in her room reading instead of doing her chores," Jim said.

"I think she read every book in the Armadillo Lake library. Never did see someone who liked to read so much." Darby's mother shook her head in confusion. "I kept telling her that reading books didn't put food on the table."

"Guess all that book-reading paid off in the long run. Look at her now—a doctor," Rosy said, smiling at Darby. "We're all so proud of her accomplishments, aren't we?"

"Sure thing," Jim grunted, at his wife's elbow jabbing his ribs.

Darby sent Rosy a grateful smile. Not that she bought her claim. Her parents would have been proud if she'd married a good ole boy straight out of school, had a half-dozen babies and farmed for a living. Becoming a doctor and living six hours away didn't even register on their "proud" radar.

They hadn't come to her graduation ceremony. Or to the opening of her and Blake's clinic.

To give them credit, Rosy had given birth that same weekend—which she'd apologized for time and again. As if she'd had any control over when her son entered the world. But Darby had never been convinced her parents would have come regardless. To her knowledge, they'd never left sweet home Alabama.

"She is an amazing woman, isn't she?" Blake turned toward her, brushed her hair away from her face, and gave her a look that turned her to melted goo right then and there on her mother's sofa.

"I can't imagine not having her in my life," he

continued, his voice low, seductive. He pulled her hand to his mouth and pressed the softest of kisses to her fingers.

Her breath hung in her throat, threatening to choke her. She couldn't pull her gaze from his dark one.

He'd been overdoing the lovey-dovey stuff all night, constantly touching her, smiling at her, looking at her as if he was visually stripping off her clothes and liking what he found.

Looking at her as if she was his whole world.

As he was doing at the moment.

Even though she knew he was role-playing, her body perked up to heights that made her mind feel a little numb and her body tingle in places she had no business to be tingling while sitting on her mother's sofa.

She'd wanted him to notice her, to be aware she was a woman, but was she really prepared to face the consequences of what she'd set into motion this weekend? Was she ready to lose what they had in hopes of winning love's jackpot?

# CHAPTER FOUR

"HEY, sis, can I talk with you a moment?"

Darby turned toward her brother, alarmed at the concern in his voice. He knew, didn't he?

"What is it, Jim?"

If any of her brothers was going to realize her relationship with Blake was phony, she'd have guessed Jim. He'd always been able to see right through her.

"I'm worried about Mom."

Both relief and concern filled Darby. "What about her?"

"She's not been herself for the past few days."

"Because of her shingles, you mean?"

Jim scratched his blond head. "Maybe. I'm not a doctor, but I think something more is going on than her rash."

"What makes you think that?"

"She hasn't acted right."

"In what way?"

"I've seen her pressing her hand to her chest and wincing."

His words caused Darby to wince. Her mother was having chest pain? "What does she say?"

"That she's fine, and I should mind my own business."

Sounded just like Nellie Phillips.

"I'll talk to her and see if I can convince her to go in for a check-up on Monday."

"I'd appreciate it. Dad doesn't say much, but I can tell he's concerned, too. Yesterday she had to come inside and lay down for a while."

"Really?"

"Yep, and she's been snapping at him."

Her mother didn't snap. She gave orders, expected them to be obeyed, and tolerated no disobeying.

"I'll corner her before Blake and I leave and find out what's going on as best as I can."

"What's going on with you and this guy, sis?

I like him, but there's something about him that doesn't sit well."

"It's probably just because he's dating your baby sister."

"Possibly." Jim glanced toward where Blake sat, surrounded by the Phillips womenfolk. "Are you serious about him?"

How did she answer? She couldn't lie to Jim. Not directly. "He's my business partner. Would I risk messing up our partnership if I wasn't serious about him?"

Her brother's mouth twisted and his gaze went back to Blake. "Possibly," he repeated. "With what happened with Trey, I don't want to see you hurt."

Darby swallowed. Her whole life wasn't measured by what had happened with Trey. Sure, she hadn't trusted a man until Blake, and that had taken years, but that was because she'd learned a valuable lesson, not because she'd been traumatized by Trey's betrayal. "That was over ten years ago."

"Ten years in which I've not seen you with another guy."

She'd dated. Rarely, and never for long enough to get close to any of them, but she had dated.

"We live in different states. You don't know how many guys I've been with." At Jim's scowl, she added, "Besides, Blake's a good guy. The best."

Her oldest brother shot another uneasy glance toward where Blake sat with the Phillips women. "He seems crazy about you."

Crazy being the key word.

Darby snapped her seatbelt and kept her smile pasted onto her face. No doubt lots of eyeballs stared out the front windows. She'd wait until they were out of sight before she tore into Blake, possibly dismembering him and tossing him into one of the chicken barns for what he'd done.

"That went well."

Darby inwardly scowled at the pleased-with-himself man pulling out of her parents' driveway. Was he insane?

Her entire family now expected her to announce that Blake was "the one", they were getting hitched, planned to buy the old Donahue place down near the lake, set up practice, and raise a family of their own.

She glanced into the side mirror to make sure her brothers hadn't jumped into a pick-up and followed them. Not only were there no head-lights, but she could barely see the house or the four long barns off in the distance.

"I'm going to strangle you," she warned, curling her fingers into tight fists.

"I thought I did better than that."

"Better? There was no reason to put on a show in front of my parents, my family. You acted like a lovesick puppy. Now they think something's going on between us."

His brows knit together and he cast an odd look toward her. "Wasn't that the idea? For me to make them think I was crazy about you? To pretend that you were my whole world?"

"No. Yes. Oh, I don't know." Clearly she hadn't thought through the consequences of bringing Blake to Armadillo Lake for the weekend. She should have made peace with

Rodney rather than hope to open Blake's eyes. Rodney was easy enough to explain away, and would have been bored to tears with her family. And would have bored her family to tears with his polished exterior.

Blake was not so easily explained away.

As her business partner, he was a part of her everyday life. After tonight's performance, her parents probably thought something had been going on between them for years.

No wonder. He'd been the perfect date—had he really been her date, that was. He'd been attentive, considerate, affectionate, had blatantly stared her brothers in the eyes, daring them to deny his right to date their sister, earned their grudging approval before the evening had ended, wooed her sisters-in-law, charmed her parents. He'd played his role too well. Way too well.

When he'd pulled her fingers to his lips and kissed them, in front of God and the entire Phillips clan, she'd had a momentary mental and physical lapse and wanted him to kiss more than just her fingers.

She'd wanted him to kiss her all over.

And she'd wanted to press her lips to his throat and kiss him. All over.

For real.

When she'd finally been able to drag her gaze from Blake's, her mother had been smiling. Not just smiling, but *smiling* smiling.

No doubt her mother was pulling out her grandmother's veil this very moment, envisioning how the simple pearl and gauzy netting would look on her daughter's head. "Finally," she'd be saying to her daughters-in-law.

Her mother would be heartbroken if she knew the truth.

"I'm definitely going to strangle you."

"You want to strangle me?" He checked for oncoming traffic prior to pulling onto the main highway that would take them the ten miles back into Armadillo Lake. "I'm disappointed. I was sure you'd be pleased and relinquish the entire top side of the bed as reward for my good behavior."

"Good behavior? Are you kidding? Do you

have any idea what you've done?" How could she look at him and not long for what they'd pretended this weekend? Not want him to want her for real? Having tasted the sweetness of his affections—even knowing they were pretend—she just couldn't envision going back into the desolate wasteland that had made up her personal life. She covered her face with her hands. "This is horrible. They're expecting us to be married by Christmas, and are no doubt at this very moment discussing what they're going to wear to our wedding."

"Why? Do they try to marry you off to every man you bring home?" He chuckled. *Chuckled.* As if he hadn't turned her life upside down with his hot looks and incessant touches. As if he hadn't just waved her parents' fondest dream in front of them—Darby married and back in Armadillo Lake.

As if he hadn't just waved her fondest dream in front of her—*him.*

"If I gave them the opportunity." She wiped her face, knowing she'd pay for tonight's show for months to come. For years. She wouldn't live tonight down until she brought home a man for real. And how she'd live this down in her heart she had no idea. Regardless of the outcome, this weekend would forever haunt her heart, her dreams. "I've never brought a man home."

That got his attention, causing him to slow down the vehicle and glance toward her. "Never? Not even Trey Nix?"

Darby sucked in air. "Trey doesn't count."

"Why not?"

She shook her head. "He just doesn't."

Technically, neither Trey nor Blake counted.

After all, they'd both only been faking their feelings for her.

Darby had washed her face, moisturized, brushed her teeth, flossed, and combed her hair. She'd put on the modest pajamas the sales clerk had assured her were sexy without looking like she was trying to be sexy.

Time to face the music. Or, more aptly, Blake in a hotel room bed. Why was she acting so crazy?

It wasn't as if he were lying there waiting for her to come to him like a virginal bride. It wasn't as if anything was going to happen between them just because he'd looked at her with desire earlier, then pretended to love her all evening.

It wasn't as if anything was going to happen between them just because she hoped with all her heart that he'd someday really want her the way she wanted him.

She gulped back her nervousness and opened the bathroom door.

Light from the television illuminated the hotel room, casting shadows and short bursts of brightness across Blake's face. He sat in the bed, all the pillows, including hers from home, propped behind his bare back.

Where was his shirt?

*Where had he gotten all those muscles?*

She'd known he had a nice body, but, oh my, she hadn't known he'd been hiding all those beautifully sculpted lines and planes. If business ever got bad, they could run an ad of Blake wearing low-slung jeans, no shirt, and his stethoscope dangling from his neck. Business would be through the roof in no time.

Her pulse was already there.

Her gaze lowered. Pajama bottoms rode low on his narrow hips. The comforter bunched at his waist, hiding everything beneath the dark navy waistband.

"I thought you'd decided to sleep in the tub," he teased, thankfully unaware of her thoughts.

"Not likely." But if a functioning spine wasn't necessary for the following day, she might grab her pillow and give the tub a shot. How could she not have known what an awesome six-pack Blake sported?

No wonder women flocked to him, were devastated when he moved on to the next beauty who caught his eye. Four years and she'd never seen the man's naked torso. Now she'd never be able to forget—never be able to look at him and not know what he hid beneath those tailored shirts.

Lord help her.

Lord help him. Because she really wanted to just tell him how beautiful she thought his body was, how beautiful she found his heart and soul, his sense of humor, everything about him.

As if sleeping in the same bed with him was no big deal, she climbed in and tugged her pillow out from behind him. "Give me that."

As if sleeping with her were no big deal, he grinned at her. "I was warming it up for you. Say thanks"

"Thanks." What he'd done was make her pillow smell of his musky scent, all spice, sandalwood, and Blake.

"I turned the air down. That okay? I sleep better when the room is a little cool."

"Fine." She didn't need a play-by-play of his sleeping habits. Really. Just knowing they were going to be in the same bed, sharing the same blankets, that her pillow smelled of him, was already playing havoc with her imagination and her will power not to roll over and jump him.

Taking a deep breath, she reminded herself of mind over matter. She could do this. She *soooo* didn't want to run her fingers over those indentions on his stomach. She didn't want to trace each outline of that six-pack. With her hands. Her mouth. Nope, she was immune to Blake's charms if all he wanted from her was sex.

She was a mighty oak that couldn't be swayed by pin-up calendar abs and spicy musk that made a woman want to deeply inhale. Not her. *Right.*

But maybe if she kept telling herself she didn't want him, she'd make it through the night without embarrassing herself.

Because she wanted so much more from Blake than just sex.

She wanted him. The whole package.

"I called the hospital and spoke with the night nurse. All of our patients are doing about the same. Dr. Kingston made a round on them this evening and introduced himself."

See, even lying there half-naked, with her on the opposite side of the bed, Blake was only thinking business. Just because she'd hoped this weekend would jumpstart their relationship into who knew what, that didn't mean he knew she'd asked him to Alabama innocently enough the afternoon the reunion invitation arrived, but quickly realized she hoped for much more.

"He plans to stop by the hospital in the morning."

"Thanks for letting me know." She'd meant to call and check on Mr. Hill and Mrs. Mayo after they'd first gotten back to the hotel room, but she'd been distracted by Blake pulling his acoustic guitar from its case. Somewhere between the country music classics she'd forgotten everything except soaking in Blake's hypnotic voice.

She tugged on the covers, tucking the material around her neck.

"You ready for the light to go out?"

Light? Oh, he meant the television. "Sure. We've got a long day tomorrow."

He clicked the remote, then put the device onto the nightstand next to his side of the bed. "Goodnight, Darby."

"Goodnight, Blake."

"Sweet dreams."

"You too.

They lay in the dark for a long time, with Darby acutely aware of each breath he took, of every movement of his body, of the fact his beautiful chest was bare beneath the sheet. All she'd have to do was reach out to feel those hard muscles bunched beneath his smooth skin.

She could accidentally brush against him. Just a quick brush of her fingertips against all that temptation.

"Why aren't you asleep?" he asked after a few minutes.

*Because now that I've seen your chest I'm not sure I'll ever sleep again.*

"Why aren't you?"

"I was thinking."

*That you should put on a shirt, because you're the stuff fantasies are made of and I'm the last woman in the world you'd want to have those kind of fantasies about you?*

"About?"

"What it must have been like growing up at your house."

*Huh?* She rolled onto her side, staring at his

barely perceptible silhouette through the darkness. "Why would you think about that?"

She felt his shrug more than saw it.

"I liked your family."

He did? Why did that cause happy bubbles to dance in her belly? Until that moment she hadn't admitted to herself how much she'd hoped Blake had liked her family.

"They liked you, too. Even if my brothers didn't know quite what to think of me bringing home a city boy."

He shifted, and she expected him to roll over and go to sleep. Instead his hand clasped hers, lacing their fingers in a warm hold that she guessed was supposed to be friendly. *Friendly* didn't cover the excited tingles working their way through her body, starting somewhere in the pit of her belly and radiating outward, sensitizing every cell along the way.

"Tell me about them."

"My brothers?" She didn't move, just lay in the bed, acutely aware of his presence, acutely aware of the fact that for the dozenth time that day he held her hand and each time he'd thrown her heart into a tailspin of longing.

"Yes."

Her brothers. Where did she start? "John and I were always the closest when I lived at home. Probably because he's the youngest of the boys and only a year older than me," she began, tugging her pillow down a bit with her free hand. "But since Jim and Rosy married, I see them most often. They usually come up twice a year to go to a football game, and they never miss the Tennessee/Alabama game."

Long into the night, they talked. She told him about her family, life on the farm, about her favorite pets while growing up. At any point she grew silent he'd ask another question, and Darby would let more of her life spill into the darkness, thinking perhaps Blake had really hypnotized her with his music. Or maybe the darkness made her feel safe in sharing so much. Otherwise she'd never be lying in bed with the sexiest man she'd ever known, holding his hand and telling him all about her crazy but lovable family, and her rather ordinary childhood, growing up on a farm, that seemed to fascinate him.

Mmm, something smelled good. Still half-asleep, Blake breathed in a deeper inhalation.

Soft, flowery, elegant, feminine.

Something felt good, too.

He shifted slightly against the warm body curled spoon-fashion with his.

In the way one does when first awakening, he became aware of his body, of the way the soft body melted against him, her legs curled against his, of the way his arm snaked around her waist, her arm lying over his, of how his palm cupped her breast through too much material.

Her head was tucked beneath his chin and the alluring scent he'd smelled was a mixture of her shampoo and her own seductive fragrance.

She fit perfectly against him, his much larger body framing hers protectively, possessively.

Not opening his eyes, he kissed the top of her head, worked his way down to nuzzle her neck, her ears. Damn, she tasted good.

Better than French fries.

Better than Darby's mom's banana pudding.

*Darby.*

He was nibbling on Darby's earlobe.

He opened his eyes, expecting her to be awake, expecting her to lash into him and tell him exactly where he could go for taking advantage of her.

He couldn't see her face, but could tell she was still asleep by her even breathing.

But even in sleep she wasn't immune to what he'd been doing. When he stopped, she snuggled into him, tightened her buttocks against him, making him bite back a groan of pleasure and need, making him want to strip off her pajama bottoms and feel her silky skin glide against him, her female to his male in all the wonders of what made the world go round.

Which was all wrong.

He shouldn't want Darby.

Only he did, naked and beneath him, moaning his name in pleasure, wrapping her legs around his waist and meeting each thrust of his body into hers with an enthusiasm that matched his own.

He tried to tell himself that his desire was due purely to circumstances—that he'd want any attractive woman he woke up wrapped around, especially one who smelled so seductive.

He laid his head back on his pillow. A man's subconscious was hell. It caused him to ignore things he didn't want to acknowledge, like what he'd wanted to do since seeing her drop those naughty undies into the drawer. But it was more than sexy lingerie. It was the woman next to him. He liked her, enjoyed her company, her wit, her intelligence, her smile, the way she challenged him to be a better man, a better doctor.

All reasons why he wouldn't seduce her. Their relationship was more special to him than giving in to sexual need. Even sexual need as paramount as what currently ailed him.

Stirring, she turned, snuggled closer, tucking her head into the crook of his shoulder, wrapping her arm over his waist and running her fingers along his belly to settle just above the waistband of his boxers.

Ah, *hell*. He should get up, take a shower—a

cold shower—anything to remove himself from the tempting lair he lay in.

But he didn't want to climb out of bed. Not yet.

Without moving his head, so as not to disturb her, he glanced toward the clock. It was still early. They'd talked way into the night and would have another late night with her reunion. He'd just let her sleep for a while longer—would pretend she wasn't who she was and that it was okay that he'd liked waking next to her more than he should have.

If not for his raging arousal that wouldn't— couldn't—be acted upon, waking next to Darby, lying with her like this, was nice.

Closing his eyes, breathing in her intoxicating fragrance, he lay next to her, willing his body under control and telling himself that any man who woke next to a beautiful woman would be reacting exactly the same way.

His mind and heart didn't race because the woman he held was Darby.

Without opening her eyes, Darby knew she was in trouble. She was wrapped around Blake like the candy shell coating on her favorite chocolate treat.

How had that happened? Obviously she'd gotten cold during the night and her body had gone in search of heat.

And Blake was heat of the hottest kind.

He was lying on his back with her cradled against him, and delicious heat radiated from the smooth skin of his chest.

And her hand.

Dear Lord, her hand was at his waist.

Not on *him*, but darn near close!

Hoping he was sound asleep, she lifted one eyelid and glanced into dark-as-sin eyes.

He was awake, and staring at her as if he wanted to see inside her head.

He *knew* she'd virtually attacked his body during the night.

"Um, sorry." Was that croaking noise really her voice? "Apparently I got cold." Trying not to appear as rattled as she was, she attempted to disentangle herself. "You make a good heater."

*You make a good heater?* What kind of stupid

comment was that? Could she please just pull the covers over her head and never come out?

"Glad to be of service," he teased, sounding quite normal and as if nothing out of the ordinary had happened, that he hadn't just wakened with her body trying to be the icing on his cake.

He wasn't going to make a big deal out of her *faux pas*. Thank goodness. Then again, he probably woke with women wrapped around his fine body all the time.

Darby didn't. Hadn't ever. Despite the fact she'd had a few boyfriends, she didn't do sleep-overs. Ever. Each time she got close, old doubts stopped her, making her question motives, making her lose all desire to risk her heart.

But who could blame her body for getting as close as possible to a six-foot-two hunk in the flesh? Especially when that flesh held the soul of a man she was willing to risk giving her heart to?

"Do you want the bathroom first?" she offered, hoping she sounded casual. She glanced toward the clock. Almost ten. They'd slept much later than she usually did. Much later than Blake slept too, since he usually went for a run in the mornings prior to his hospital rounds.

The picnic started at eleven.

In an hour she'd face her high school nemesis and the boy she'd once planned to give her virginity to. She'd be alongside a man pretending to love her and doing such a great job he'd thrown her internal circuits off kilter and was feeding her dreams of what it would be like to really be loved by him, both physically and emotionally.

Enough so that she'd almost throw caution to the wind and take whatever kind of relationship Blake would give.

A quickie relationship would cause everything between them to sour. But what if he really could fall in love with her? What if they could be both business partners and lovers?

"Let me go, real quick, then the bathroom is all yours."

Quick. Quickie. Heat burned her face. Had he really just said "quick"?

She tried not to look as he slid out from

beneath the sheet. More and more of his flawless chest and abdomen were exposed. She tried to tear her eyes away from the arrow of dark hair that disappeared beneath his boxers.

Boxer briefs. She'd thought his waistband had been to pajama bottoms or shorts. "You wore underwear to bed?"

She'd slept with Blake. In his underwear. When she'd awakened she'd known there weren't many barriers between their bodies, had felt his hairy legs tangled with her smoothly shaven ones, but she'd thought he'd been wearing more than his underwear.

Stretching his arms over his head, drawing attention to the lean planes of his body, he lifted a dark brow. "Is that a problem?"

How dared he look so hot first thing in the morning? She'd wanted to see him ruffled, but she hadn't meant like this, with sleep softening his expression, his hair sexily tousled, his body barely covered with brief cotton boxers that left little to her imagination.

"Yes, it's a problem! You're not wearing

underwear to bed tonight. Not if you expect me to be in that bed with you. Got it?"

His lips twitched with amusement. "Okay. If you insist. I wouldn't have last night if I'd known how you felt."

Scowling, Darby crossed her arms over her breasts, trying to hide her body's reaction to his stretch, to his near nakedness, to his comment that she knew was only his usual teasing.

"That's not what I meant, and you know it."

"Hey." He put his hands up in mock surrender. "I was just trying to follow orders. You know I like it when you're all Darby bossy."

"Fine, let's see how you do with *this* Darby bossy. Hurry up in the bathroom, because as you can tell—" she gestured to her make-up-free face and sleep-mussed hair "—I've a lot of work to do before we go to that picnic, and I don't want to be late."

Why miss a single moment of reminiscing over the most humiliating time of her life, with the man of her dreams there to watch?

# CHAPTER FIVE

Mandy Coulson wasn't what Blake had expected.

She was petite, blonde, curvy, brown-eyed, and had a friendly smile that appeared genuine.

From the way Darby acted each time her name was mentioned, he'd been looking for horns and a pitchfork.

However, when she glanced toward Darby something did shift in her gaze. Something Blake couldn't completely read. Guilt? Regret? Anger? Resentment? Or maybe Mandy wasn't looking at Darby at all, but rather the man chatting with her.

Trey Nix.

Blake stood a little taller, held his head a little higher. And attempted not to spy on where

Darby talked to the man whom she blushed at with every other word he said.

Damn it. *Blake* was the only man she blushed for. Didn't she know that?

He hadn't realized until that moment, but it was true. Darby didn't blush at any time except when he teased her as he had this morning.

She'd blushed like crazy when he'd climbed out of bed.

But she was also blushing right now, while smiling at something a man from her past said while he looked at her as if he'd like to take a big bite of her future.

Who was the guy, and what had their relationship been?

Based on what little Darby had said, on what her family had alluded to the night before, he'd guess they'd been romantically involved and Darby had been hurt.

"How long have you and Darby been together?" Mandy asked, glancing toward where Darby spoke with Trey. Her brown eyes narrowed at the talking couple.

No doubt about it. There had been a love triangle between the three of them.

Also glancing toward where the tall man flirted with Darby, Blake didn't like the direction his brain was taking him, nor the fact that looking at her blushing for another man made him feel caught up in a triangle of his own.

Which was crazy.

He and Darby didn't feel that way about each other. Even if going to sleep holding her hand and waking next to her had been unexpected pleasures.

"We met in medical school. The moment I saw her I wanted her."

He said the words as part of his madly-in-love-with-her role, but hearing the confession out loud sent cold chills over his body.

He *had* wanted Darby the moment he saw her.

He had been denying that want for years, because she wanted different things from life than he did, but the want was there all the same. It had definitely been front and center this morning, when he'd awakened holding her, wanting to do much more than that.

"She's a lucky girl."

Mandy's words had Blake's gaze returning to the woman, but only for a second. He didn't like how Nix had backed Darby against the widest tree Blake had ever seen, how his hand rested above her shoulder and he leaned in while talking to her.

More than that, he hated how Darby looked at the man, with rosy color high on her cheeks. Had she forgotten she'd arrived with him? That they were supposed to be together?

Pretending to be in love or not, no woman he arrived with was going to flirt with another man during their date. Hell, no.

"Excuse me."

Without waiting for Mandy's response, he went to interrupt Darby's tête-à-tête with the past.

Darby leaned back against the wide base of the oldest oak tree in Armadillo Lake. The rough bark digging through her clothing, she regarded the man who'd once devastated her teenaged heart.

"You grew up to be one fine-looking woman."

Trey grinned at her, his green eyes twinkling just as they always had.

He hadn't gained fifty pounds, lost his sandy-blond hair, nor lost the good-looks that had won more hearts than just her naïve teenaged one. Other than the more pronounced crinkles at the corners of his eyes and mouth, he looked like the same old Trey, sounded like the same old Trey. The only thing that had changed was that he didn't elicit the same old heart-fluttering meltdown in her chest that he once had.

She didn't feel anything for him except anger that he'd treated her so shabbily all those years ago. Anger that burned her cheeks, made her curl her fingers into her palms to keep from slugging his grinning face.

His grin was all wrong, and it didn't reach his eyes—eyes that were the wrong color. His grin didn't lift his laugh lines just so, didn't make her want to smile back.

Not like the man she'd awakened with this morning—the man who did put her fluttering heart into meltdown in ways Trey never had, not even during the heyday of her high school crush.

Not like the man who was now chatting up Mandy. *How could he?*

She smiled up at Trey with more enthusiasm than she felt. "Um, thanks."

"Everyone was wondering if you'd be here." He rubbed his knuckles across her cheek.

"They were?" Nothing. He was touching her and nothing was happening. No flutters. No silly schoolgirl giggles in response to his attention. No desire to have him take her into his arms and kiss the fire out of her. No desire to hold his hand and talk long into the night. *What was Blake talking with Mandy about? Why was Mandy smiling?*

"Yeah." He grinned again. "They were taking bets down at the Piggly Wiggly."

Heat flooding her cheeks, Darby's gaze shot to Trey. She blinked. "Bets?"

"On whether or not you'd show. High school doesn't exactly have good memories for you."

He'd played the star role in those bad memories.

For years she'd carried a crush for him, had dreamed of him noticing her, and when he had his attention had merely been to get back at Mandy.

"High school was a long time ago." Just look how much smarter she was these days. Then again, considering who her heart pitter-pattered for these days, maybe she wasn't nearly as smart as she'd like to think. "Besides—" she forced a smile to her face "—the reunion was an excuse to bring Blake home to meet my parents."

His eyes momentarily darkening, Trey's grin kicked up a notch. "You could invite *me* to visit with your folks sometime. It's been a while since I've seen them. Your Mom still the best cook in town?"

"Yes, she is—and perhaps you've forgotten, but the last time I invited you it didn't go so well."

"I was young." He laughed, as if his explanation made everything okay. He reached out, cupped her jaw, and stared down at her. "If I'd been half as smart as you were, I'd have held on to you."

"Obviously you weren't that smart—but I am." Blake took Darby's hand. Unmindful of how close Trey stood, he pulled her to him, knocking the other man's arm away with the force of his tug.

Darby blinked at the menacing way Blake glared at Trey, at the possessiveness in his dark eyes when they shifted to her.

It took her a moment to recall he was just playing a role, that he was fulfilling his "crazy about her" part. That he wasn't really jealous.

With that, Blake's head lowered, his mouth brushing over hers in what could only be called a staking-his-claim kiss.

His kiss wasn't gentle, wasn't a caress.

His kiss was a branding of his mouth against hers—a kiss meant to say she belonged to him and none other.

Darby's heart pitter-pattered.

No, that wasn't a pitter-patter. That wild beat was a thunderstorm, a horrendous onslaught on her senses, complete with lightning and thunder and raindrops that pierced her soul.

She let her fingers thread into his hair, tangle in the silky locks, pulling him closer, loving the solid strength of his body against hers. Her mouth opened and his tongue thrust inside, imprinting her with his kiss, stamping her as belonging to him.

Dear sweet heaven, she'd never been kissed so thoroughly and completely and all-consumingly. Blake kissed her as if she really was his, as if he really was ticked that another man had been making moves on her. As if he'd fight to keep her at his side. He was kissing her as if he wanted her, loved her.

The way she'd dreamed of being kissed by him.

Only he was faking.

She knew it, and so did he.

That knowledge gave her the power to pull away, the power to smile at Trey and give Blake an annoyed look.

"Blake, please, we're at a family picnic." Unsteady, she placed her palm against his chest, surprised to find his heart doing a rapid pitter-patter of its own. Still, she pushed against him, trying to establish space between their bodies.

His gaze narrowed, his thumb raked across his

lips, removing the last trace of her lipstick. His eyes never left hers, never lost their steely possessiveness, never lost the dark swirls of desire that looked so real they took her breath away.

"Let's ditch the picnic and go back to the hotel, Darby."

"Just for the record," Trey drawled, leaning against the tree and watching them, "I'm a lot smarter these days."

Darby's gaze cut to him. She hadn't even remembered he was there. She blinked, sure she must still be asleep and having some weird dream.

Maybe when she woke up she wouldn't want to take up Blake's pretend offer to head back to the hotel. Because at this moment she wanted to. For real.

If she believed he was sincere, they'd be out of there.

Having followed Blake, Mandy stepped up beside them. "Good for you, Darby. I'm glad you've met such a great guy and won't die a virgin, after all."

Heat burning her cheeks, Darby rolled her

eyes, sure Mandy meant the words as some type of dig, knowing Mandy had meant her to be embarrassed in front of Blake.

Blake's forehead wrinkled with a frown, his gaze going back and forth between Mandy and Darby. "What's she talking about? Dying a virgin?"

"Nothing, really." Mandy laughed, the sound sparkly. "Just one of those silly 'most likely' predictions kids make."

"Most likely?"

Mandy smiled. "Darby's was…"

Darby opened her mouth, tried to speak, tried to stop Mandy from saying it out loud, but words wouldn't come from Darby's mouth. Mandy's mouth had no such problems.

"Most likely to die a virgin."

Would the ground please open up and swallow her? Or lightning strike the tree and drop a branch onto Darby, knocking her senseless? Either would work. Just so long as she didn't have to look into Blake's eyes and see the pity there, see the realization that she'd been a loser in high school.

Blake's arm snaked around Darby's waist, keeping her close. "I can put that ridiculous prediction to rest."

"We noticed." Mandy giggled, fanning her tanned face. Her brown eyes twinkled at Blake. "If the thermometer wasn't reading over a hundred before, it is now. That was some kiss."

Mandy was right. The temperature must be triple digit, because Darby was melting from Blake's heat. His arm burned through her thin clothes, making her sweat.

"That kiss was nothing," he promised, making her wonder if he'd read her mind. "Not compared to what Darby and I share. She'll die a well-loved woman." He stared down at her, his eyes sparkling like gleaming black onyx. "As long as there's breath in my body, I'll see to that."

Darby stared at Blake in awe.

She could kiss him.

Not just because Mandy's jaw had dropped, not because Trey looked at him with something akin to envy, not because he'd just single-handedly saved her face over the past humiliations she'd suffered, but because in that moment, when he looked at her, she believed him.

Which was exactly why she needed to make sure she never kissed Blake again.

Because none of this was real.

Not his kiss, his looks, or his words.

Because Blake was faking and she was the idiot who'd asked him to. The idiot who had to keep reminding herself that none of this was real, no matter how much she wished it were.

She'd set a dangerous game into play, having Blake pretend to love her. A game she wasn't sure she could continue.

Thirty minutes later, Blake wondered if the people of Armadillo Lake were too blind to see the person Blake saw. Their lack of vision had damaged Darby's self-confidence in ways he hadn't realized.

But how could he have? She'd always come across as so together. So self-assured. So confident in who she was.

Only here, in a place that stripped her of the

armor she'd so carefully shielded herself with, did he see the vulnerability in her eyes. The need to belong, to be accepted, to show that, despite whatever had happened in her past, she was somebody worthy, both then and now.

Darby had something to prove, and he couldn't help but wonder if that need went far beyond making a statement with an impressive "date".

He wanted her, caught glimpses of desire in her eyes, had felt her desire in their kiss, but did she really feel desire for him? Or just gratitude for his role this weekend?

"Blake, are you going to play softball with us?" she called, from where she stood with a couple of females who wore friendly faces and seemed to genuinely be glad to see Darby. He'd liked the women—their husbands, too.

"Maybe he doesn't want to get his city-boy butt whooped by a bunch of country boys."

Trey Nix he didn't like.

Had Darby really had a relationship with that strutting buffoon? Former high school star quarterback or not, the guy was a self-absorbed loser. One who'd taken a look at present-day Darby and decided to make up for lost time.

Over Blake's dead body.

He hadn't played softball ever, but he'd once been a hell of a Little League baseball pitcher. Too bad they'd moved away near the end of the season, cheating him out of sure tournament victory. After his third unfinished season due to frequent moves Blake had opted not to play another organized sport, but he had played the occasional pick-up game at the fancy prep school he'd attended.

He wasn't sure that would keep him from getting his butt whooped, but even if he'd never gripped a bat before he wouldn't back down from the challenge in Nix's eyes.

Five innings later Blake was thinking perhaps he should have recruited a few of his old Little League teammates. His current team was losing by two runs, and he was up to bat with a runner on base. With the right hit, he could tie the game.

Before Blake's first pitch was thrown a loud wail had everyone's heads turning toward the playground near the park's pavilion.

"Bobby?" called a woman Blake had seen re-peatedly with Mandy, while the other two women stared toward Darby, talking low. The woman abandoned her third base post to rush toward her crying son. "What's wrong?"

The game forgotten, the rest of the team made their way to where the boy lay on the ground, clutching his arm.

His broken arm.

"What happened?"

"He fell when he jumped from the swing," another boy informed them, his little face a mixture of curiosity and fear.

"Didn't we talk about not jumping from the swings?" But even as she said the words the woman's face paled, tears clouded her eyes, and she hugged the boy to her.

Blake started to step forward to check the boy, but when Darby bent next to the mother and son he reached for his phone to call for an ambulance.

"Someone bring a bag of ice for Bobby's arm, pronto," she ordered. Smiling, she placed her hand on the boy's hand. "Hi, Bobby. My name is Darby Phillips, and I'm a doctor. Can I see your arm? I'll be gentle."

Obviously terrified, the boy shook his head, burying his face into his mother's chest.

"Bobby, honey, let her check your arm." Whatever differences were between them, the woman obviously had no problems with Darby examining her son. "She's an old friend of Mom's and Aunt Mandy's."

Nor with distorting the truth.

Although not happily, the boy let Darby check him.

While explaining to the ambulance service what had happened, Blake watched Darby assess the boy's arm, admiring the way she spoke with him, explaining what she was doing in that calm, controlled voice.

Trey handed Darby a plastic bread sack that had been filled with ice and knotted at the end. Darby shot him a quick look of thanks and placed the bag on Bobby's arm.

"Although the skin isn't damaged, both the radius and the ulnar bones are broken, just proximal to the wrist." Darby glanced at the woman. "I suspect the bones will need to be surgically pinned."

"I could drive you." Trey spoke up from where he stood next to her still, obviously eager to come to the rescue.

Blake opened his mouth to tell the guy to get lost, that he was on the phone with the emergency service and an ambulance should be on its way soon. But Darby took charge.

"Could you? That would be great. You drive us in Cindy's vehicle, so she'll have transportation at the hospital." Darby gave him a smile that had Blake's insides crawling. "Blake will follow us, and you can ride back with us."

Great. Just what Blake wanted—to chauffeur Darby and her ex. Why were they going to the hospital anyway? They couldn't do anything except keep the arm stable. An orthopedic surgeon would be required to correct the damage to the bones.

But if Darby wanted to accompany the boy to the hospital, he wouldn't argue. The whole weekend was about her, for her, and he'd agreed to play by her rules.

Even if he'd quickly realized he didn't like those rules.

"I'm going, too," Mandy piped up. "Cindy might need me."

Darby's expression tightened, but she didn't say anything, just turned her attention back to Bobby.

Listening to the emergency dispatcher, Blake whistled. Darby was right. The closest emergency service was thirty miles away and wouldn't arrive in Armadillo Lake anytime soon. They could get the boy to the hospital faster than waiting for the ambulance.

"Let's go."

# CHAPTER SIX

FRESHLY showered, Blake sat on the hotel room bed. Humming to himself, recalling how Darby had clung to his every word the night before when he'd sung for her, he pulled on his black Italian shoes.

They'd gotten back from Pea Ridge about fifteen minutes earlier. They'd stayed at the hospital with Cindy, Mandy and Trey until Bobby had been admitted to a room on the surgery floor. He'd have surgery early the following day, to pin the broken pieces of his ulnar and radius bones.

As Darby had gone into the emergency room with Bobby and the boy's mother, Blake had been left in the waiting area with Mandy and Trey. That hour had been one hell of a long wait.

Making Blake happier than they could have possibly realized, Mandy and Trey had stayed at the hospital, rather than ride back with them.

On the drive home, Darby had looked spent and closed her eyes. He'd encouraged her to lie down on the bed to rest while he took his shower. When he'd come out of the bathroom she'd been on the phone, not surprisingly, and was firing question after question about what was going on at Knoxville Memorial Hospital regarding their patients.

When finished, she clicked her cellular phone closed. "I called and checked in with Dr. Kingston. He discharged Evie Mayo this morning, along with both of your patients."

His patients had been simple dehydration cases, so he wasn't surprised they'd been released to go home. He'd expected as much. Darby didn't sound sure about her patient.

"You don't think he should have discharged Evie?"

"We still don't know why her liver enzymes

were so elevated. He says they've dropped to below a hundred and she was fine."

Blake had reviewed the woman's chart, examined her, and hadn't been able to offer Darby any suggestions other than perhaps the woman had an unusual virus. Her white blood cell differential had been slightly shifted, with an increased lymphocyte count, indicating the possibility of a virus.

"Evie was okay with the discharge?"

Darby shrugged. "He says she was ready to go home."

"He's a good doctor."

"Yes." Glancing at her watch, she nodded. "I should get ready. Thank goodness we only have to go downstairs."

She stood from the ornate chair, gathering her clothes to take into the bathroom with her.

"Darby?"

She turned, her gaze colliding with Blake's.

"Are you going to tell me what happened between you and Mandy before we go downstairs?"

She shook her head.

"How about what happened between you and Nix?"

"We're going to be late if I don't get my shower."

He sighed. He'd hoped she'd tell him last night, but she hadn't. She'd seemingly shared everything with him except whatever her connection was to Trey and Mandy. "When you're ready to talk, I'm here for you."

Before turning her back on him, she smiled, but it didn't reach her eyes.

"I know," Darby said. Blake had always been there for her. Not that she'd needed him often, but when she had he'd been there without hesitation. Like when she'd had the flu. He'd not only covered for her in the office and at the hospital, but he'd brought her a basket full of edible goodies and stayed with her in case she'd needed anything.

Her hand on the bathroom doorknob, she paused, spun to face him. "Why are you so good to me, Blake?"

His dark eyes clouded with confusion. "What do you mean?"

"Why are you here with me this weekend? Surely you had better things to do than go to my high school reunion?"

"You blackmailed me, remember?"

Her grip tightened on the doorknob. "Blackmailed?"

"Blackmailed might be a bit strong," he admitted, humor evident in his voice. "I owed you a favor so I'm here."

Pretending to be in love with her, so she wouldn't lose face with people from her past who didn't matter anymore. Why had she thought they had? Why had she given them such power over her life? Why had she let Trey's rejection impact her so much?

But somewhere along the way her reasons for keeping the opposite sex at bay had shifted from fear of rejection to waiting for Blake to notice that she was a woman, that they made a great team.

Only he never had, and she'd tired of waiting.

The kiss they'd shared flashed through her

mind, lighting fires just at the memory of Blake's intensity. When she'd joined him in the waiting room his gaze had dropped to her lips. Had he been remembering their kiss? Or had he been pretending for Mandy and Trey's sakes?

*"Oh, what a tangled web we weave when first we practice to deceive."*

Biting into her lower lip, she sighed. She'd asked for this. Asked for him to pretend. What was that old saying about being careful what you asked for?

"I would have come anyway, Darby, if you needed me." His gaze searched hers. "Do you regret my being here?"

He'd seen more of her than any other man, had seen the real her, and he'd stood back and let her handle Bobby's injury this afternoon, knowing she'd needed to handle Bobby's care, to prove something to herself and to her hometown.

Inherently, Blake knew her. Sometimes he knew her more than she knew herself. He helped her see things more clearly. Helped her to feel more confident about herself, about the woman she was, and about who she wanted to be.

He helped her to trust the opposite sex, because Blake was the only man she trusted who wasn't blood kin.

"No, I don't regret you being here. Far from it," she admitted honestly. She trusted Blake more than any person she knew. With her business, her reputation, and with her past. "You're a nice man, Blake Di Angelo."

"Nice?" He coughed, sputtered, and snorted amidst laughter. "Don't you believe it, Dilly."

She rolled her eyes at the nickname he'd likely never let her live down. But, despite his antics and intentional teasing, she'd spoken the truth.

Nice? Darby thought he was *nice*?

Blake shook his head, picking up the remote to flip through the television stations, pausing to watch the world news, expecting any moment to see headlines flash: "Dr. Blake Di Angelo accused of being a nice guy. Truth soon to be revealed and partner to dump his sorry butt."

Because the last thing he was feeling in regard to Darby was *nice*.

He'd established that first thing that morning, and nothing had happened during the day to persuade him otherwise.

Darby was a wonderful woman, the best he knew, but their relationship was a strictly no-sex one. Not that they'd ever discussed sex—they hadn't. Not in regard to them having sex. There hadn't been a need.

He'd done his thing, she'd done hers, and the twain had never met.

But all his thoughts currently featured Darby, and no matter how many times he told himself to quit thinking of her in sexual terms his libido refused to cooperate.

Nice? She thought he was *nice*?

Surely after that scorching kiss they'd shared he rated more than "nice"? That kiss had practically had smoke curling from his fingers and toes and she called him a nice guy? What the—?

When the bathroom door opened, Blake was still fuming. He wasn't a nice guy—didn't want

Darby to think of him in that light. Which begged the question, how *did* he want her to think of him? Had he wanted that kiss to start fires inside Darby? Had he wanted her to see him as more than her business partner?

Glancing toward the door, he felt his body answer his question for him. He wanted Darby to want him, hoped his kiss had curled her toes and put stars in her eyes.

He wolf-whistled. Her hair was swept up in a fancy do, exposing the graceful lines of her neck. The blue dress clung in all the right places and sent his libido into hyper-drive.

And her shoes. Had he ever seen her in heels like those? Sexy black stilettos with a wide ankle strap that begged for a man's touch. He visually traced his way over her legs. His tongue stuck to the roof of his mouth. She was so tiny, but her legs went on and on. The heels pumped out the firm muscles of her calves, tightened the sliver of her quads that showed beneath the hem of her dress.

"You look amazing."

First turning, to give him the full effect of her

outfit, unknowingly hardening him to mammoth proportions, she rewarded him with a smile. One that lit her eyes to sparkling blue gems and softened the fullness of her all too kissable pink lips.

"Thank you." Her gaze skimmed over his black pants, matching jacket, the blue shirt she'd suggested, and silver diamond-patterned tie. "You don't look too shabby yourself, City Boy."

Unable to drag his gaze from her, he drank in every delectable inch. "Let's forget the reunion and stay here, so I can prove to you how not nice I am."

Because her *nice* comment stung. What guy wanted to be described as nice?

Laughing, she rolled her eyes. "Be serious, Blake."

He was serious.

He wanted her. Enough that he was tempted to push her onto the bed, push up that silky hemline, remove whatever skimpy, groan-worthy scrap of silk she was wearing, and kiss her until she begged him to take her.

Which drew him up short.

This was Darby, not some flavor of the month. Despite the fact he'd been pretending to be in love with her all weekend, he wasn't. Acting on the sizzling attraction he was feeling toward her would ruin their business relationship, would ruin their friendship. A smart man would remember that.

Standing from the bed, he sighed with an exaggerated heave of his chest, determined to keep the mood light. She had enough on her plate tonight without having to deal with his unwanted sexual attraction. "If you refuse to stay here and let me see how few seconds it takes to get that dress off you, then let's go before I do my best to change your mind."

Her eyes gleaming with delight, she moved to the end of the bed. Her hips swayed, courtesy of her heels. "You're good for a girl's ego."

"That's me. *Nice*, and an ego booster."

"Don't make my compliment sound like a bad thing," she admonished, checking her appearance in the mirror. "It's not."

"Because that's how every man wants a beautiful woman to think of him. Nice, and her personal ego-fluffer."

She laughed nervously, smoothed her hands over her skirt. "We're alone, Blake. You don't have to say things like that."

He eyed her curiously, wondering at her uneasiness. "Like what?"

"That I'm beautiful." She looked away, pink tingeing her cheeks. "Or that you want to get me out of my dress. You don't have to pretend when we're alone. Actually, I wish you wouldn't, because when you do I start believing things that aren't true."

Pretend? Was she kidding?

He walked around the bed, lifted her chin to force her gaze to his. Staring down into her blue eyes, he resisted the urge to kiss her until there was no doubt about what was pretense and what wasn't.

Instead, he stroked his finger along her jawbone, caressing her delicate features. He turned her toward the dresser, toward their reflection in the mirror. He stood directly behind her, close enough to feel her body heat, close enough to tease his senses with the brush of her dress against him. He was so hard he hurt, but this wasn't about him. This was about Darby.

Even with her high-rise shoes, she barely came up past his chin, but they looked good together—her blonde, blue-eyed perfection next to his dark Italian features.

"Look in the mirror, Darby," he urged, his gaze locked with hers. "See the woman I see. She's beautiful. Every red-blooded male is going to envy me tonight because they'll all know you'll be coming back here with me." He placed his hand on her bare shoulder, his fingers stroking over her soft skin, toying with the thin blue spaghetti strap of her dress. "You are a beautiful, intelligent, witty, desirable woman, and any man would count himself lucky to know you. I do."

Wordlessly, she stared at their reflection, her eyes big, blue, searching his. She swallowed, inhaled a quick breath, and her lips parted. "Blake, I—"

He couldn't breathe, thought he might suffocate at the heaviness that had come over his chest with his admission, with the way Darby was looking at him with a mixture of confusion and desire.

In that moment he knew he had to get out of the hotel, away from the queen-sized bed that called to him. He had to get air. Now.

Otherwise he'd forget thousands of years of human refinement, go Neanderthal, scoop Darby into his arms, and take what his every instinct dictated he possess.

"Come on, Dilly." He grabbed her wrist. "Let's go get this charade over with."

Before he forgot to be nice and was as bad as he wanted to be.

"We sure could use a doctor in town," the slightly overweight brunette intoned, giving Darby a dramatic look as they talked over the band playing Lynyrd Skynyrd in the background. "Just think what might have happened to poor Bobby's arm if you hadn't been here. Cindy said the doctor told her what a great job you did splinting his arm. Thank goodness you were here."

Darby smiled at Leah. They'd known each other since grammar school, but had never been close friends. The closest friend she'd ever had had stabbed her in the back. Over Trey.

"I second that," a tall, nice-looking man said, stepping up to where they talked. He shifted his beer to his other hand and stuck his hand out to her, then to Blake. "Mark Lytle—nice to meet you. Hey, Leah."

Darby shook his hand, trying to place him in her memory and coming up blank.

Seeing her confusion, he grinned. "I'm the local vet—moved here from Texas a few years back when Doc Tatum retired."

"Mark Lytle," she repeated, the name registering. She recalled her family mentioning him.

"I'm here with Debbie Earnhart. She's working the registration desk," he said, a friendly smile on his face. "Although it's definitely outside what I was trained to do, I'm forced to take care of minor human problems more often than you'd believe. Tell me how I can convince you to set up practice here."

Darby didn't say anything at first. Mostly because she didn't know what to say. She'd spent most of her teenage years wanting to get away from Armadillo Lake, yet in this moment she struggled to remember why, when her home-town really did need better access to healthcare. Her own mother would have to go out of town to have her shingles checked, and Carla had almost delivered in the back seat of John's truck because the closest doctor had been miles away.

"If I ever decide to relocate, I'll keep your offer in mind." Hopefully hiding her discomfort, she smiled. "Did you buy out old Doc Tatum's vet office?"

As she'd hoped, the conversation turned to Mark's animal health clinic. Several other couples joined them.

Blake stayed close to her side, attentive to her every need. His palm pressed low on her back in both possession and in reassurance that she could do this, had nothing to fear, and that he thought she was beautiful.

He didn't have to say the words again.

She could see the truth in his eyes when he looked at her. Blake thought she was beautiful. On that, he wasn't pretending.

That alone kept a smile on her face, made her aware of his nearness at all times.

They made conversation with couples, ate buffet-style finger foods, and mingled—but all the while sexual tension sizzled between them, arcing higher and higher each time their gazes met, each time their fingers brushed against the other.

Tension that had been slowly building from the moment she'd asked him to pretend to be in love with her. Tension that had twisted her body into knots at waking curled against his body. Tension that had mounted during his possessive claim of her mouth under the oak tree. Tension that threatened to explode if he didn't quit looking at her as if he wanted to lick her from head to toe.

A commotion at the front of the room had Darby glancing that way. Mandy and Trey. Together. Homecoming Queen and King. Head cheerleader and star quarterback. Former best friend and former major crush.

For weeks she'd thought the sight of seeing them would be like taking a bullet to the heart. Surprisingly, she'd felt more regret over wasted time and heartache. During high school she'd lost her best friend—and over what? A guy. Okay, so when she'd been sixteen Trey had seemed like much more than just a guy, but what had she known back then? Not much.

Funny how time changed things.

Like her relationship with Blake.

Because this weekend *had* changed things between them.

When he'd kissed her earlier she'd burned right down to her toes. She'd dreamed of him kissing her for years and now he really had. When she'd stared at her and Blake's reflections in the mirror she'd wanted him to kiss her again. She wanted him to kiss her now.

She wanted Blake in a way she'd never wanted anyone. She'd been attracted to him for years, but had always known he was a playboy at heart, had wanted more than what he gave to other woman. She'd settled to have him as her friend and partner, something he had reserved just for her. But this weekend, having his attention targeted on her, having him look at her with love in his eyes—well, she'd started believing the lies and wanting Blake's heart, wanting it badly enough that she wondered how she'd ever go back to the way things were if that was what Blake wanted.

"Darby?" He followed the direction of her gaze, cupped her elbow a bit too tight. "Are you okay?"

"I'm fine," she lied, knowing that if she ruined her relationship with Blake she'd never really be fine again. "I wasn't expecting to see them together."

Which was better than saying, *I wasn't expecting to want you even more than I already did—wasn't expecting to believe in your pretense of loving me since I know that's what it is—wasn't expecting to want to throw caution to the wind just because I can see you really do want to have sex with me.*

When Mandy's gaze connected with Darby's, she made a beeline toward them. Her glittery gold and brown dress hugged her trim figure as she smiled and waved. "I want to thank you for what you did for my cousin's little Bobby today."

Keeping a forced friendly expression plastered on her face, Darby nodded. "You're welcome. How is he?"

Mandy stood, looking gorgeous, but also equally awkward.

"Asleep." She sighed, giving a little shake of her beauty-salon-styled hair. "Cindy is with him. As part of the reunion committee she did a lot of work, trying to make this shindig a success. She shouldn't miss out on everything when Bobby is so sedated he won't know whether she's there or not."

Had it been *her* son lying in that hospital bed, Darby wouldn't have left him.

Her son?

Her blood pooled at her feet, leaving her light-headed. Where had that thought come from? Medicine had been her dream, the only one she'd ever given serious thought to after Trey. So why were there suddenly visions of dark-eyed, dark-haired toddlers dancing through her mind?

Mandy prattled on, looking almost as if she wasn't sure what to say next. She kept her smile in place, kept talking in her sweetest Southern twang. "But look at you." She motioned to Darby. "You always did want to be a doctor and now you are one, and you knew just the right thing to do when Bobby fell. You must be so proud."

Darby expected a "bless your heart" to hit her any moment. Why was Mandy being nice?

Unsure of her swirling emotions, Darby started to take a step back, but Blake's hand kept her in place, burned through the material of her dress, singeing her with reassurance that he was there if she needed him, that she needed to stand her ground.

Was she misreading the hope in Mandy's brown eyes?

"I only left the hospital a little while ago—had to get my hair done." She glanced at the blonde bangs hanging over her eyes. "The doctor said you did a fantastic job caring for Bobby. We were lucky you were here. You really should come home."

Armadillo Lake did need a doctor. Desperately.

But not her.

After a too-long silent stretch, Mandy gave a little wave of her fingers, and shot Blake an overly bright smile. "Well, I should mingle. After all, I was student body president and I am supposed to be the hostess."

Unsure what to think about the exchange, Darby watched Mandy blend into the crowd.

"Unbelievable," Blake breathed close to her ear. "She was trying to talk to you, and you cut her off. It's obvious she has regrets."

Turning toward him, Darby scowled. "Have you forgotten what she did to me?"

"No." His dark eyes cut into her. "I can't forget, because you won't tell me what she did. Why did you cut her down?"

Was he yet again taking Mandy's side? Were men so easily fooled by a pretty face? Was she forever to have her date defend Mandy? Would Blake leave the prom—the reunion—with Mandy, too?

Moisture pooled in her eyes, threatening to spill down her cheeks. She wouldn't cry. Not because of the past. Not because of whatever emotions ran through her, making her want to cling to Blake and beg him never to leave her, to never destroy her trust the way she'd been shattered at sixteen.

Which she would never do. Never again would she be so humiliated, so hurt by a man.

Not even Blake.

"Why don't you just butt out of things that aren't any of your business?" she bit out, needing to put distance between them, needing to lash out at the sting she'd felt at his defense of Mandy. She spun to go in search of something to drink, and bumped into Trey near the bar.

"Hey, babe." He took a swig from the bottle of beer he held. "That was cool of you today with Bobby."

Still brewing over what Blake had said, she absently waved off Trey's praise. "It was no big deal—just what I do."

"Yeah, but not something most people can do—save someone's life. I'm impressed."

She blinked up at him. "I quit trying to impress you years ago." She hadn't really, she realized. Because every man she met, every man she dated, she saw through the pain she'd suffered at Trey's hands, saw without being able to trust in their words, their feelings for her.

"I've always felt bad about what happened." He glanced down at the drink in his hand, picked at the silver label with his fingernail. "But I didn't know how to tell you I was sorry. I wanted to, thought about it a million times, but finding the words to apologize for something like that wasn't something I seemed able to do."

"A simple 'I'm sorry' would have done."

"I'm sorry." He grinned, and she had a flash of remembrance of what she'd found so appealing about him. "Forgive me?"

Trey had only asked her out to get back with Mandy. It had worked. Whatever differences had split them up, when Mandy and another guy had pulled up to the lookout point, overlooking the lake, Trey, Darby's date—the guy she'd been making out with, planned to go all the way with—had jumped out of his car, punched Mandy's date and made up with her, leaving Darby to find her own way home.

"To be honest," he continued, "you scared the hell out of me. You were so smart, and knew exactly what you wanted out of life. I liked you, but felt like a goofy kid next to you." He sighed. "Then there was Mandy."

Yes, there had been Mandy—who had fallen for Trey at the same time Darby had. They'd idolized him from afar for years. When they'd been fifteen, Trey had fallen for Mandy. In the fallout, Mandy had dumped her friendship with Darby. It had only been when his relationship with Mandy had gone sour that he'd asked Darby out.

"I loved her, you know." He gave a self-deprecating shrug. "I admit what I did to you was wrong, was a sorry thing to do, but I never meant to hurt you that night."

No, he'd only meant to take everything she'd been willing to give—her virginity, her love, her wide-eyed trust—and then walk away the moment he and Mandy worked things out. Which they'd done.

Still, looking into Trey's sincere eyes, she did believe him. He'd been seventeen and a typical teenaged boy. Was it his fault she'd taken his loosely spoken words of affection to heart?

"Okay, I believe you didn't intentionally hurt me."

"Great. Let me buy you a drink. Friend to friend."

They weren't friends, and likely never would be. But her emotions were ragged from Mandy, Blake, and even from Trey. From the whole weekend. What would one drink hurt? It was what she'd come over here for, needing to escape the disapproval in Blake's eyes. He'd sided with Mandy. Didn't men always side with the Mandys of the world?

She shot a quick glance toward Blake. He sat at their table, his expression as dark as his eyes. He didn't have to crook his finger for her to know he wanted her back at their table, away from Trey. Not this time. This time her date would come to her, would claim her.

She lifted her chin and smiled at Trey. "Why not? I think you owe me a few."

"That I do." His gaze raked over her face and he grinned lazily. "And I intend to pay up in spades."

For the second time that day Blake interrupted Trey Nix making moves on his woman. "I'm cutting in."

"I don't want you to cut in," Darby argued, clinging to Nix's shoulders.

"Quit lying. The only reason you're on the dance floor is so I'd cut in."

Blake had stayed in the background, letting

her stew on what had transpired between her and Mandy and come to realize she'd been the one to ask him to butt into her business by pretending to be in love with her in the first place.

Butt out of her business? Had she forgotten who'd invited whom?

He'd watched her down drink after drink with her first love, watched her glare defiantly, daring Blake to come get her, then flirt with Nix. He'd forced himself to wait for her to come to her senses, to be patient, but when she had gone into the other man's arms on the dance floor Blake had had enough, and butted into her life yet again.

Darby frowned.

Blake frowned right back, tugging her with enough force to unplaster her from Nix on the dance floor.

"Darby?" Trey said, lines creasing his forehead.

"Hold on a minute, Trey." She held up her fingers, then turned to Blake. "Maybe you should go find a friend to dance with and leave me alone."

"No more games, Darby. We both know who

you came with tonight, and who you're leaving with. Me." He pulled her to him, holding her close so there was no doubt about who he meant.

"Are you so sure about that?" Her eyes flickered with annoyance, then softened, a smile curving her lips. "Did you just growl at me?"

He glanced into her happy eyes—eyes that made him want to dive into their unknown blue depths. "I growled. So sue me."

"You're a doctor—you should never say that," she warned, laughter spilling from her painted pink lips as she waved goodbye to Nix, where he still stood. Her gaze returned to Blake and she wrapped her arms around his neck. "Should never offer things you don't mean. Someone might take you up."

He inhaled her sweet scent. The fresh, light floral fragrance had been teasing him all night, making him want to lean in, making him hungry. Starved.

"You should never rub against a man who wants to kiss you, because he might take you up on your offer."

She stopped moving against him. The slightly dazed look in her eyes said she hadn't realized what she was doing, but then she smiled. "What took you so long, Blake? I thought you were never going to rescue me."

What had taken him so long? Rescue her? "You were the one who told me to butt out of your life," he reminded her, still more than a little irate at her blatant flirtation with Nix.

"I didn't mean it," she repented, without hesitation. Her eyes took on a serious hue, shone up at him with wide-eyed sincerity. "I want you in my life. Always, Blake. Just you."

His stomach somersaulted, making his insides churn. Just him. Noting the tremble in her lower lip, the fruit on her breath, he stared closer. Another growl rumbled from his throat. "How much liquor did that jerk ply you with?"

"Liquor?" She blinked, tightening her arms around his neck, laughter in her eyes as she toyed with the hair at his nape. "Trey didn't give me liquor. Just punch." She licked her lips. "Mmm, it was good. Best punch I ever had."

He might have laughed at her innocence if her pink tongue tracing over her lips hadn't put his entire body into a vice, hadn't grabbed hold of every nerve cell and demanded full attention.

"You're drunk, Darby. I should take you upstairs."

"I'm not drunk." She stared at his mouth. "But take me upstairs, please." Her long lashes brushed her cheeks. "What would you like to do to me first?"

Blake almost tripped over his feet. A million different items volleyed for first place in the "what he'd like to do to Darby" list. He wanted to do them all. He wanted to act on each and every vivid thought in his head. With Darby.

He gulped. "Maybe going back to our room isn't such a great idea."

Darby's lower lip pouted. "Why not?"

He tried to laugh off the way he felt, as if he didn't believe she was serious. "I might take advantage of you."

"Isn't that the idea?" Her fingers tightened in his hair. She stood on her tiptoes and looked deep into his eyes, her expression inviting. "Let's go. Take advantage of me. Now."

There she went, getting Darby bossy again.

Didn't she know that turned him on? That *she* turned him on? More than any woman. Her earlier words seared through his mind. She'd told him to butt out of her life. Words that had cut deep. Words he should heed rather than the ones she currently shot at him. A smart man *would* butt out of her life.

"You don't know what you're doing."

"Yes, I do." She tugged on his hand, moving against him in a slow sway. "I want to make love with you. *Now*."

She spoke loud—loud enough that the couples around them heard and snickered.

"Guess we know for definite that Dilly didn't die a virgin."

Blake wanted to assure them Darby was the *least* likely woman to die a virgin. But, although Darby had occasionally dated, she'd managed to keep each of the boyfriends at arm's length, never really letting them close, finding faults in each that allowed her to remain in control.

He'd always admired her control. Now he wondered if her control had been a safety mechanism, a way of making men butt out of her life when they tried to get close.

He suspected he knew more about her, that he was closer to her than any man she'd dated, and until today he'd never so much as kissed her. *Was she a virgin?*

The idea was impossible for his brain to wrap around.

No way was the hottest woman he knew a virgin.

Still, the possibility struck him and he couldn't let it go—no matter how many times he tried to dismiss the notion as ridiculous.

"Are you?"

She rested her head against his shoulder, swaying in rhythm with him on the dance floor. "Am I what?"

"A virgin?"

Still punch-happy, she smiled up at him, her eyes starry, her lower lip pouty, begging to be kissed. "If I was, would you promise to save me from my 'most likely' curse?"

# CHAPTER SEVEN

DEAR Lord, had she really just asked Blake to make love to her? To save her from her virginity?

Darby giggled to cover her nervousness.

She was nervous. For the first time she'd asked a man to make love to her. Not just any man, but Blake Di Angelo—the man she'd been waiting for her entire life.

Because she loved him.

Had always loved him.

"Is that what you want, Darby?" His hands brushed across her cheek, cupped her face so he could study her so intently she wondered what he saw. "For me to make love to you?"

More than her next breath.

Calling upon every ounce of courage she possessed, she stretched, tentatively touched her mouth to his, hoping to show him as words couldn't convey just how much she wanted him.

Would he push her away? Tell her she was crazy? That he couldn't want a woman who was more brains than beauty, who was so the opposite of the women he usually dated?

She tasted the soda on his tongue, tasted the masculinity that was pure Blake. Eyes wide, she deepened the kiss. He let her set the pace, but his rapidly hardening body was far from immune to her kisses.

He pushed her into a darkened corner of the ballroom, lifted her chin. "I want you, Darby. Tell me you want me to make love to you because you want me and not because you're drunk."

She barely registered when the music stopped, the lights brightened, and Mandy spoke into a microphone.

"I'm not drunk." She pulled back, smiled softly up at him, her fingers twisted in the hair at his nape. Lord, how she loved his hair. How she loved him. "I want you. Take me to our room and make love to me."

Blake's black eyes narrowed, his body tensed, and Darby wondered if she'd made a mistake. Had she lost him forever with her boldness? In admitting so much of her heart? He'd said he wanted her, too. Surely he wouldn't be frightened away by her honesty in telling him what she wanted? Namely him.

Or was Blake like Trey? Were his words loosely spoken during make-out sessions? Uncertainty flooded her. What if he didn't really want her? If he'd realized she could never be good enough? What if they made love and she couldn't please him? What if he decided he liked her better for her brains than her body? She wanted Blake to want both. The whole package. All of her.

Please, God, let him love her.

Because, no matter what the cost, no matter what the consequences, tonight she was laying her heart on the line. Because she didn't want to be just Blake's business partner or his friend. She wanted him. As her lover. As the man who wanted to share his life with her. Always.

If they weren't meant to be, she didn't want to go through life without knowing, without having taken that chance at grasping her dream.

Because in that moment her biggest fear was never taking that risk with Blake, never knowing *what if...?*

His jaw shifted. "You're sure?"

"More sure than I've ever been about anything." She was. She didn't want to continue pretending that she didn't love him when she did. She didn't want to pretend her heart didn't race when he walked into a room. She didn't want to pretend not to want to spend every moment of her life with him. Unable to guard her heart, she stared at him, willing him not to hurt her. "Please want me, too."

"I do. More than you'd believe." He cupped her face, kissed her so thoroughly she thought she might melt. He grabbed her hand. "Let's go, Dilly."

"About time, City Boy," she quipped back, practically running to keep up with his long strides out of the ballroom.

Nervous excitement fluttered in Darby's belly. Tonight she was going to give herself to Blake and take whatever he was willing to give of himself.

The elevator door slid shut, locking out the world. He stared straight ahead, not looking at her.

"Blake?"

"Not now, Darby," he barked, startling her into taking a step back.

She wilted. This had all been a bit of a fantasy. One that she should have known better than to believe. "You've changed your mind?"

He turned, scorched her with his hot black eyes. "Unless you want me to wrap those long legs of yours around my waist and take you right here in the elevator, and the world be damned, I advise you to stand over there, look pretty, and be quiet."

Her lips rounded in a surprised "O". Why had she doubted him? Been so quick to think he'd changed his mind? That she'd be lacking in his eyes?

She wasn't sixteen anymore. She was a grown

woman who knew the man she wanted and was wanted back by that man. She wouldn't doubt him again.

She took a step closer to him, displaying a smile on her face and a great deal of leg.

Blake shut the hotel room door, taking Darby in his arms immediately. She tasted good. Like a tall drink of water—and he was a man dying of thirst.

If the elevator hadn't dinged that they'd arrived at their floor the moment it had, they likely wouldn't have gotten out.

Her fingers curled into his hair, tugging him closer, urging him to kiss her more deeply. Her body squirmed against his, pushing him to the edge of sanity.

When her tongue slid between his lips and into the recesses of his mouth he fell. Deep. Hard. Swiftly. Fell into an abyss that was only him and Darby and the intense passion burning between them.

He wanted to be inside her. Had wanted to be inside her all evening. All day. Forever.

A warning rang in his head. A warning he would usually have listened to, but not tonight. Tonight he was going to have Darby. All night. Every way. She was going to be his.

Darby was his.

Tomorrow he'd worry about the consequences. About the nagging voice that kept saying he shouldn't do this.

Tonight was his, to explore her body, to kiss every inch of her, to commit every nook and cranny of her body to memory.

Tonight he'd know what it felt like to drown in the blue of her eyes, to lose himself in her smile, to taste the sweetness of her skin, thread his fingers into the long tresses of her thick hair, and to know Darby belonged to him.

She stared up at him, her eyes hazy, her lips swollen from his kisses. "Love me, Blake."

With her demand, she reached for his belt, undid the catch with amazing speed and pulled the leather strap free from his pants. Her fingers curled around the belt.

He clasped her wrists, took the belt from her

with ease. "Slow down, babe. We're not in a hurry."

Although he longed to reach the finish line, this was one race he planned to savor every step along the way.

With a clang, his belt landed on the bureau.

He turned back to the most beautiful woman he'd ever known, the most seductive. Slow and tender, he claimed her mouth, capturing her sigh of pleasure.

"Blake…" she murmured against his lips. She pushed at his jacket, dropping it off his shoulders and down his arms. He stepped back to let the jacket fall to the floor.

Her gaze locked with his, she undid the buttons of the blue shirt that matched the exact shade of her desire-filled eyes. A shirt he'd bought for that very reason—because the color reminded him of her. When she'd undone the last button, she tugged the material from his waistband, brushed her hands over his chest and removed his shirt.

Bare-chested, standing in his dress pants, he

waited to see what she'd do next. He wasn't disappointed.

She ran her fingers along his abdomen. Sighing in appreciation, she bent, pressed her lips to his sternum, his collarbone, his throat. She rained kisses over his goose-pimpled flesh until he could stand no more.

"I want to taste you, Darby. Let me."

"All you had to do was ask." She turned, presenting her back for him to help remove her dress.

Inch by torturous inch he lowered the zipper, revealing more and more of her creamy skin, more and more of the black strapless bra. When he reached the indention of her low back, he pushed the blue spaghetti straps from her shoulders, slid the dress down her hips and let the material puddle at her feet.

She stood in the skimpy black underwear and garters he'd fantasized about only the night before, wearing heels that made her legs endless and his fantasies eternally grateful.

He swallowed, knowing her image was forever burned into his brain, knowing he never wanted to forget the way she looked or the desire for him in her eyes.

"You're beautiful." His voice rasped like that of a schoolboy, but he was thankful sound came forth at all, considering how thick his throat had grown.

"Thank you."

"I mean it, Darby." He ran his palms over her arms, laced his fingers with hers. "You are beautiful."

"So are you." Her gaze raked over him, reinforcing her praise, making him even harder.

She stepped into his embrace.

She tucked her head beneath his chin, wrapped her arms around his neck, and swayed to a tune that only they could hear.

He moved with her, each sway of their bodies exciting him more, each kiss, each touch building the momentum of what was to come.

His hands moved lower, trailing along her spine, cupping her bottom through the black silk. He lifted her to him, hip to hip, his hardness pressing into her softness. The contact wasn't enough. He needed to be closer to her, needed to be inside her.

With him supporting her weight, and her arms wrapped around his neck, she raised her legs, pressing snugly against him, encircling his waist.

His legs turned to water and, not wanting to drop her, he moved forward, sitting her on the bureau. Her legs remained around him, the juncture of her body pressed enticingly against his groin. They kissed, over and over, touched, explored each other's bodies in hungry greed.

Blake undid the back clasp of her bra, freeing her breasts, taking a taut nipple into his mouth.

"Oh, Blake, that feels good. So good," she moaned, arching her spine toward him.

"It's going to feel better."

"Promise me you won't stop," she begged, her hands cupping his face, forcing him to look at her. "Ever."

"I'm not stopping, Darby. Not tonight. Not ever." Why would she think he'd stop? "Unless this isn't what you want?"

"*You* are what I want."

He'd never heard sweeter words. A rumble

caught in his throat, emerging as a low growl. "As long as you want me, I'm yours."

Darby couldn't believe how bold she was. Blake might have been right when he'd said she was drunk. She certainly felt light-headed, intoxicated. Intoxicated, but amazingly powerfully feminine at the same time.

Blake's body responded to every caress of her fingers, to even the lightest touch of her mouth against his flesh.

Never had she imagined a man could be so in tune with her thoughts, her body, her desires. Never had she imagined she'd be so able to read how her touch made his skin burn, how her mouth triggered heat deep in his gut.

Knowing Blake wanted her as much as she wanted him was the most amazing feeling of her life.

He scooped her into his arms, carried her to the bed, and jerked the comforter back. He laid her down, kissed her, removed a condom packet from his wallet, and shed his pants with lightning speed.

She'd been right. He was beautiful.

"I want to make this good for you."

Didn't he know that as long as it was he who touched her, this would be good?

He unhooked her garters, slid her panties from her hips, pausing to kiss her thighs, her knees. Careful not to tangle the material on her heels, he pulled the scraps of black silk free from her body, then kissed her again. All over.

Holy smoke. How could a kiss light so many fires?

Fires that raged burning hot. How could his fingers trailing over the same places cause such tingling? Such liquid heat at her very center?

He was torturing her with his slow touches, his purposeful seduction of her senses. She wanted him. Inside her. Making her whole.

Pulling on his shoulders, she tugged him to her, locked her mouth with his, rotated her hips beneath him in a seductive rhythm. His body matched it, grinding against her, above her, pinning her beneath him, pressing her into the bed.

He slipped on a condom. Then he was filling her, breaking every barrier, stretching her body to accommodate his girth.

She muffled her cry of pain into the curve of his neck, dug her fingers into his shoulders, and prayed he didn't notice.

"Darby," he groaned, staring down at her with concern in his black eyes. "You weren't really a virgin, were you?"

"I'm not a virgin," she promised, not wanting him to stop, afraid he would. Afraid she wouldn't feel the ultimate pleasure his kisses, his fingers had promised would be hers with their consummation. She raised her hips, taking him deeper, moving her body against him, feeling pain give way to the pleasure she sought, welcoming the electricity spreading through her inner thighs.

She hadn't lied. She wasn't a virgin.

*Not anymore.*

Darby's head throbbed, her eyes burned, and her muscles screamed in protest at the night's activities. Her lips felt bruised, and she'd tossed her head back and forth to the point she'd never get the tangles from her hair.

Still, she smiled as she stretched.

What an amazing night. She ached in places she hadn't known she could ache. A good ache. Like when you'd run a marathon and won. Like when you'd been made love to over and over by a man who couldn't get enough of you.

She had.

Sweet and tender, hot and fast, Blake had claimed every inch of her body.

She'd done some claiming, too.

She smiled at the memories. Blake's groans of pleasure at her touch, his worshipping of her body and his teasing her awake with kisses when she'd thought she was too tired for more. She'd been wrong.

Not bad for a beginner.

With the way Blake had held on to her afterwards, she'd say not bad at all. They'd been good together. She didn't have to have experience to know they'd shared something special.

Was it because she loved everything about him? His eyes, his smile, his spicy scent, his pin-up abs that she'd licked every indention of, his intelligence, his…? Oh, she loved him. Enough said.

Rolling onto her side, she opened her eyes, ready to wake him and tell him every emotion in her heart. Instead she looked into black eyes.

Black eyes that were filled with regret. And guilt. And more regret.

Her elation fizzled like a deflating balloon that lay lifeless on the ground.

"Don't even say it," she warned, putting up her hand to shield herself from his recriminations. She didn't want to hear about how he regretted what they'd shared, didn't want him to make the most beautiful night of her life something cheap, shabby, wrong.

"Say what?"

As if he didn't know.

"What I see in your eyes."

"And that would be…?"

"That you think last night was a mistake."

Maybe it had been a mistake, but, wow, on the scale of one to ten last night had been an eleven. An amazing *hallelujah* eleven.

He lay back on his pillow, stared at the ceiling, and ran his oh-so-talented fingers through his hair. "You were a virgin, weren't you?"

She couldn't tell him. Not with the angst already lacing his voice. Didn't he understand that she'd awakened wanting to love him forever, not face recriminations?

"I'm not a virgin, Blake, but until last night with you Trey was—" She stopped, knowing by the way Blake's head snapped toward her that she'd said the wrong thing.

"Trey?" Sitting straight up, he spat the name at her. "You slept with Nix? Is that what you meant to say? That he was the only man you'd slept with until last night?"

"No." She hadn't meant to say that. She'd meant to say that there hadn't been anyone she'd ever cared enough to have sex with except Trey, and Trey had been a silly schoolgirl crush.

"Don't lie to me, Darby."

She might have told him the truth—that, had he wanted her innocence, she'd have given her virginity to Trey on the night of her junior prom. But Trey had left her willing body to go to Mandy. She might have told him that every time she'd gotten sexually close to a man she'd backed away because she'd heard Mandy's voice telling her she'd die a virgin, and she'd wondered at her reasons for being with whatever man she'd been with since she hadn't loved any of them. The moment she had that thought she'd always stopped, and usually ended the relationship soon thereafter.

Last night she hadn't had any such thoughts. All she'd known, thought, *everything* had centered around the man lying next to her.

She'd been consumed one hundred percent by Blake.

But she bristled at his tone, bristled at the way his nostrils flared and the pulse hammered at his throat.

What right did he have to judge her if she *had* stupidly slept with Trey all those years ago? It wasn't as if Blake hadn't slept his way through enough beauties to fill a little black book—a big black book, for that matter.

"Just because we had sex it does not give you the right to suffocate me."

"Suffocate you?"

"Like Rodney," she accused, knowing Blake wasn't the only one who knew how to push buttons.

His nostrils flared. "Well, apparently you didn't sleep with Rodney, or any of the other guys you've dated during the time I've known you."

"No." Had the covers just shifted lower on his abdomen? How could she look at those flat planes and long to touch him during the middle of an argument? How could she want him so much after three times during the night?

"Why not?" He moved, and the sheets barely covered vital parts.

"Because I didn't want to." Please don't let the sheets slip lower. Not if she was to keep her sanity, her cool.

He punched his pillow, bunching the foam

underneath him. He regarded her for several long seconds. "Why me?"

"Because…"

He stared at her, his expression as black as his eyes. "Was it was because of him?"

"I have no idea what you're talking about."

"Because Nix turned you on last night? Is that why you slept with me? Was sleeping with me some type of revenge?"

Was he crazy?

"Our having sex had nothing to do with Trey." Far, far from it.

"Right." He sounded angry. "We've known each other for a couple of years and nothing like this has happened. Throw loverboy into the picture and within twenty-four hours we're going at it. You can't tell me that's coincidence."

She could tell him lots of things. Like how hurt she was that he'd launched into an argument first thing that morning, when she'd been filled with such giddiness at what they'd shared.

"Believe what you want. I don't care." Okay, so she cared. Too much.

She had to get out of there now. Before she burst into tears. She swung her legs off the bed, hating that she was naked, but having no choice other than to pull the sheet around her toga-style. Somehow the thought of doing that made her feel more vulnerable than her nudity. To hide her body would be admitting she had something to hide.

How could she have thought of Trey when the man next to her consumed her every thought? The usual voices, the usual doubts—they hadn't come. Only she'd come. Time and again, in Blake's strong arms.

Shouldn't she be the one with regrets? Blake should be an old pro at mornings after. This was her first. Surely there was something wrong with his being the one upset?

Of course she knew what the differences were. She'd been making love to him, and he'd been having sex with her.

Big difference.

This morning, first thing, he'd started a fight. Why? To put distance between them? To keep her from getting ideas that last night had meant something to him beyond sex?

Her back to him, she stood from the bed. Before she took a step, he grabbed her arm, pulled her back into the bed. "Where do you think you're going?"

Super-conscious of her nudity, she toppled onto him, her breasts squashing against his bare chest, making her even more aware of her lack of clothing. "Let me go."

His gaze locked with hers, he wrapped his arms around her, pinning her to him. He shook his head. His nose rubbed against hers more by accident than design. "Not until we finish this conversation."

"I don't want to talk to you." She wiggled against him, trying to free herself. After only a few seconds she realized all she was doing was turning them both on. He'd grown amazingly hard against her belly.

She'd grown amazingly hungry to feel him inside her.

Truth was, she'd awakened wanting him.

Had that been why he pulled her into bed? Because, despite whatever recriminations he had, he wanted her too? Had that been why she'd half-heartedly fought for her freedom, moving against his naked body with her own?

"Darby?" Her name came out on a low growl from deep in his throat. Desire shone in his eyes. Desire for her.

Her gaze lowered to his mouth. Soft, and full of the ability to give her pleasure. Maybe he was right. Maybe they did need to talk before this went further.

"Kiss me," he demanded.

"No." She wanted to, but somehow she held out. Somehow found the strength to pull away from him again. Probably from the hurt she felt at the regret she'd seen in his eyes. How could he look at her like that and then ask her to kiss him as if nothing had happened? They couldn't have sex again if he was only going to regret it afterwards.

"Yes." He lifted his head, straining to meet her lips, but Darby held just out of his reach.

In a quick roll, Blake pinned her beneath his long frame. His eyes dark, filled with fire, he lowered his mouth to hers, kissed her deeply. Kissed her until she was breathless and clinging to him, until she burned from the inside out.

"I want you, Darby."

"You said we needed to finish our conversation," she stubbornly reminded him, scared of how much she wanted him.

"Maybe we don't need words to communicate," he murmured against her mouth, his gaze locked with hers, waiting for her acquiescence. Why was she fighting him? Even if she never had anything beyond this day, she'd have this moment in time when Blake had wanted her. He must have seen the capitulation in her eyes, felt the softening of her body, because he claimed her mouth, body, and soul.

For the next half-hour, they didn't need anything but each other. Words would only have gotten in their way.

# CHAPTER EIGHT

FRESHLY showered, and finished packing the last of her belongings from the hotel closet, Darby frowned at the number on the cellular phone in her hand.

Jim. Was he calling to invite her and Blake to her mother's Sunday lunch? Her mom always cooked big on Sundays, so the entire family could gather after church services. Darby had called and checked on her yesterday, but guilt slammed her. She should have gone by prior to the picnic.

Now, the last thing she wanted was her family witnessing whatever was happening between her and Blake. She hit the answer button on her phone anyway. "Hey, what's up?"

"I know you're probably already headed out

of town, but I think you need to check on Mom."

The hotel room door opened and Blake stepped into the room. He'd carried his bag down to his SUV and come back for hers. His gaze met hers, but quickly glanced away. No smile. No wink. Just regrets. So far today, in bed, their bodies tangled together, was the only time he'd seemed comfortable with her.

"Why?" she asked her brother, watching Blake move around the room, checking to make sure they hadn't forgotten anything. "Is her shingles bothering her more today?"

"Dad called to say she didn't feel well and could I feed the livestock. I stopped in to check her after finishing."

A cold chill of premonition ran down Darby's spine. "And?"

"She doesn't look right. Her skin is pale and she keeps clutching at her chest. She says she can't catch her breath, and when she stands she feels like she's going to pass out. She's barely been off the sofa all morning, but she refuses to let me take her to the hospital in Pea Ridge."

Darby's blood ran cold. "Call the emergency services. Give her an aspirin. I'll be right there."

Blake tossed Darby's bags into the back of the SUV.

"Since I know the way, I'm driving." She held out her hand. "We'll get there quicker."

Although he'd have preferred to drive, especially with Darby looking so shaken, he didn't argue, just handed over his keys and got into the passenger seat.

He understood she needed to be doing something. Anything. He'd felt similar emotions when he'd been six and his grandfather had died. Wasn't that when he'd decided to become a doctor? When he'd watched his mother, crying over his grandfather's body, neither of them knowing what to do?

Throughout his aimless, spoilt life that had been the one constant: his desire to become a doctor.

His mother hadn't understood. His grandfather had been a wealthy man, had left that wealth to his daughter and grandson. To his knowledge, his mother had never worked a day in her life, just flitted from city to city, from one social scene to the next.

Blake had hated the constant moving, never having roots. But for the first time in his life he'd awakened this morning understanding his mother's drive to move. He'd wanted to pack his bags and take off and not have to face what he'd done. What he'd ruined with Darby.

A night of sex—damn good sex—would lead them into troubled waters that were sure to prevent them from ever returning to their former relationship.

The fact he'd taken her virginity—and he knew he had, despite what she'd said and his momentary lapse of blinding jealousy over Nix—complicated things even more.

Darby had been a twenty-eight-year old-virgin and he'd taken that from her. What the hell had he been thinking? He should have stopped the moment he'd realized.

He shouldn't have been in a position of realizing.

She was his partner, his friend, his colleague. He'd had sex with her. Now what? What would she expect of him? She'd acted as if sex between them was no big deal, but he'd seen the hurt in her eyes, felt that hurt rip into his gut. What did that mean? What did he want it to mean?

What he wanted to do was go back to the point where she'd asked him to come with her this weekend and take his answer back. Surely he could have come up with a few thousand reasons why he couldn't go to Alabama this weekend?

Darby honked the horn at the car in front of them. Despite the solid yellow line, she swerved into the other lane to pass the car.

He braced himself by holding onto the dashboard. "You're not going to do anyone any good if you run off the road."

"I'm not going to run off the road." She didn't bother looking at him, just continued to fly down the highway.

He stared at her pale features, fighting the

need to reach out and touch her, to offer comfort. "You're trembling."

"So?" she asked, leaving part of his tires on the pavement when she rounded the turn to take them up the long drive to her parents' farm.

So he wanted to comfort her. But knew he wouldn't. After last night, this morning, he needed to put distance between them, to steadfastly work on restoring their former relationship.

Maybe if they cooled things down, pretended nothing had happened, eventually they'd get back to where they'd been, back to what Blake knew had been the happiest time of his life. Why had he ruined everything by taking her to bed?

Last night had been amazing, the best sex of his life, but no sex was worth losing Darby. Deep in his gut, he knew he'd lose her before all was said and done, and he wanted to howl in frustration at his stupidity.

The SUV came to a jarring stop as Darby braked hard in front of the house. Without waiting for him, she jumped out of the vehicle and ran up the steps, across the wide porch, and into the house.

Blake got out, opened the rear of the SUV, and pulled a black doctor's bag from beneath the back seat.

What met him when he entered the house had his heart dropping to the soles of his shoes.

Nellie Phillips lay on the living room floor, her family huddled around her. Darby was straddling her, doing CPR on her chest, tears streaming down her ashen cheeks.

Oh, hell.


*Please don't die, Momma. Please don't die.*

Darby begged over and over as she used all her strength to compress her mother's chest, as she blew life-saving breath into her mother's mouth.

Vaguely, she was aware of Blake dropping down next to her, rummaging in his bag, and withdrawing a syringe to inject her mother with adrenaline.

"Let me do the compressions."

Although her arms had turned to jelly she didn't stop, couldn't break her rhythm.

*Don't die, Momma. I'm here.*

She couldn't stop for even the briefest of seconds to let him take over. But when she bent to give her mother a breath Blake replaced her hands with his, compressing her mother's chest.

Wanting to collapse from the mental and physical strain, Darby gave her mother a breath every fifth compression Blake made.

As if in a dream, she heard her brothers talking, heard Rosy crying, heard her father's fearful voice. Her gaze went to Blake, watched him compress her mother's chest, his muscles flexing with each attempt to restart her mother's heart.

In a haze, she breathed into her mother's lifeless mouth. Praying. Wanting to cry. Wanting to be the daughter. Not the doctor trying to save a life.

*Breathe, Momma, please breathe.*

"See how far away the emergency services are," Blake ordered. "Tell them we need them here stat. We need a damned defibrillator."

"They've sent a helicopter," Jim said, holding

a crying Rosy to his side even as he talked into his cellular phone.

But they didn't have a defibrillator.

Her mother's heart wasn't beating and they didn't have a defibrillator.

Darby's own heart hurt, wanted to burst from the pressure inside it.

No, her mother couldn't die.

*Please, God, please don't take her. I need my Momma. I didn't know how much, but I need her in my life.*

"I have a pulse, Darby. I have a pulse," Blake practically shouted, sounding almost as relieved as the feeling washing over Darby.

Her mother sputtered, sucked in a ragged breath.

Darby kissed her forehead. "Breathe, Momma, take another breath. I need you to take another breath."

Darby thanked God when she felt the light breath from her mother's nostril blow against her skin. "She's breathing. Oh, Blake, she's breathing."

He nodded, easing his compressions. She

checked her mother's breathing while he checked her heart-rate.

"Respirations are ten."

"Pulse is fifty-six," he said, at almost the same time.

Too low, but a big improvement over not at all.

*Please, Momma, hang in there. Just keep breathing.*

The whir of a helicopter could be heard in the distance, and Darby's inner sigh of relief shook her entire body.

"Pulse is fifty-two," Blake said. "Thank God the helicopter is here."

Her mother's eyes fluttered open; she looked at her. Her lips moved, softly speaking, but Darby couldn't make out what she said.

She leaned forward. "What is it, Momma? I'm here."

"Home." Was the only word Darby could make out. "Home."

The flight paramedic rushed into the house, took a quick history from Blake and Darby, while another paramedic put in an IV and administered medication.

"There's only room for one of you to ride in the copter with us."

Darby wanted to go with her mother, but glanced toward her father. He looked ill himself, as if little of his lifeblood pulsed through his pale body.

"Go with her," he said, his voice rumbling with emotion. "Go with her and take care of her for me."

Darby nodded, wanting to hug him, but knowing the paramedic wouldn't wait for her.

"I'll drive your father to the hospital, Darby," Blake said.

"Or he can ride with Rosy and I," Jim spoke up from where he stood next to their father.

Darby didn't wait to see how they worked out the logistics of who was riding with whom. She rushed out of the house, staying next to the stretcher that carried her mother, and with each step she took her prayers grew more and more fervent.

They'd gotten her mother's heart restarted, but had they been too late? Had she suffered brain damage from lack of oxygen? Would her heart be strong enough to keep beating?

Torn in a thousand directions, Blake laced his hands with Darby's, knowing she wouldn't stay seated on the waiting room sofa for long. She'd paced almost non-stop. But he wanted her to know that no matter what had happened between them the night before, this morning he was here for her. He hated what she was going through, and wished he could take away her worries. He gave her a gentle squeeze.

Her gaze dropped to their hands. Surprising him, she scooted closer and laid her head against his shoulder.

Fighting the panic rising in his chest, he wrapped his arm around her, pulling her close and taking her hand back in the opposite hand.

She needed him right now. In ways that had nothing to do with their having had sex. She needed him as her friend and colleague. It was okay if he held her, comforted her. It was no more than he'd have done even if they hadn't spent the night having sex.

"Thank you," she said softly. "I don't know what I'd have done if you hadn't been with me, Blake."

He understood. He had felt as if he was six years old again when he'd stepped into the room and seen Darby's mother lying on the floor. Only this time he'd known what to do. Just as Darby had.

"You'd have done everything that needed doing. Just as you always do," he assured her, knowing it was true. Darby was the most capable woman he'd ever known.

"I felt so helpless, so weak, as if nothing I was doing made any difference," she whispered, so low he barely heard her.

"You saved her life, Darby."

"We both did." She sucked in a deep breath. "I'm glad we were here."

"Me, too," he agreed, although the truth was he wished he'd never stepped foot in Armadillo Lake, never crossed lines that shouldn't have been crossed. But now wasn't the time to deal with his recriminations. Not when Darby's mother fought for her life. Right now Darby needed him, and he'd be here for her. Once they were back in Knoxville he'd deal with straightening things out between them. "Armadillo Lake needs a doctor."

"She can't die, Blake. I couldn't bear it if she died." Darby's eyes closed, her body tensed, but she didn't say anything else.

He glanced up, his gaze meeting Darby's oldest brother's blue eyes. Jim didn't say anything, just took in how Darby leaned against Blake before nodding his approval.

Would her brother be nodding if he knew Blake had stolen his sister's virginity? That he'd taken something precious from her? Him, a man who used women for pleasure, gave pleasure in return, but never wanted anything more.

His stomach churned with guilt. Darby deserved better than what he offered women. She deserved roses, romance, and happily ever after. Things Blake had no reason to believe in, much less any desire to give.

Her entire family was in the waiting room now. Jim had called his brothers, and most had met them at the hospital. He'd driven his father and Rosy to the hospital. Blake had followed in his SUV.

"She's going to be okay, isn't she?" Darby spoke low, and Blake understood the reasons why. All day she'd been strong, had been the one fielding her family's questions. Only with him did she feel she could let her guard down enough to show the slightest weakness, the slightest fear.

Her raw pain caught him in the solar plexus.

"Yes," he answered, hoping he told the truth. Darby's mother had suffered a myocardial infarction and, according to the emergency room physician, was currently being examined by the cardiologist on staff. Blake stroked Darby's hair, kissed the top of her head. "She's going to be fine, sweetheart. You'll see."

Blake willed that to be the case, trying not to wince at his use of the endearment. In that moment he'd have done anything to keep her from hurting, anything to comfort her and give her happiness, and quite frankly that scared the hell out of him.

"Darby, we need to talk—"

"Oh, Darby, I just heard about your mother." Mandy Coulson and Trey Nix entered the waiting area. "Bobby had his surgery this morning," Mandy continued, before any of them could say a word. "Trey and I have been with Cindy, waiting in his hospital room. We stepped out to get a drink and ran into Carla. She told us everything."

Darby tensed in Blake's arms. Because of Mandy? Because of Nix? From desire? Hating the jealousy flowing through his green veins, Blake tightened his hold.

"I'm sorry to hear about your mother, Darby," Nix said, standing awkwardly near them.

Darby pulled loose from Blake's arms, straightened, smiled at the couple. "Thank you. That's sweet of you."

Sweet? Blake scowled.

"Is there anything we can do?" Mandy stepped closer.

Darby shook her head. "I don't think so."

Mandy's gaze lowered, then she nodded, as if

in understanding of Darby's cool tone. "We'll keep her in our prayers."

Darby stared straight at Mandy, her expression unreadable. "Thank you."

The cardiologist stepped into the waiting room and all eyes turned to him.

"Mrs. Phillips has suffered an acute MI, but thus far isn't showing any major residual damage. She's going to be admitted for observation. I'm going to do an arteriogram in the morning, but overall she's a very lucky woman."

Everyone breathed a sigh of relief.

When the cardiologist left the waiting area, Darby couldn't resist looking to see if Blake had noticed the amount of tan flesh on display beneath Mandy's Daisy Dukes. Her gaze collided with his dark one.

He'd been looking at her. Why?

She couldn't read his thoughts—wished she could.

Had she really spent the night in his arms, opening her body and her heart to him? Feeling as if their souls were connected? Could one really share something so beautiful with a person and not know what to say mere hours later?

He leaned back in the uncomfortable waiting room chair, eyeing her as if she were an anomaly. No doubt she was. He dated a certain type of woman, and she wasn't it.

Her throat tightened. What was going to happen to them? Why did she even care? What was most important was that her mother was going to be okay. Still, she couldn't look away from Blake's dark eyes, couldn't help but wish he loved her.

She'd leaned on him, but she'd felt his tension, felt the awkwardness in the way he held her. Everything had changed between them and it made her sick. The entire day made her sick. First what had happened with Blake, and then her mother.

"I need some fresh air," she said, to no one in particular.

Blake stood as if to follow, maybe to confront her over what had happened between them, or maybe he'd seen the longing in her eyes and wanted to nip those thoughts in the bud.

Rising from where she sat with Trey, Mandy grabbed her hand. "I'll go with you."

*Huh?* Darby stared at her former friend, wondering why she could possibly want to go with her.

Darby didn't say anything, just left the waiting room.

"I'm glad your mother is going to be okay," Mandy said when they stood outside the emergency room entrance.

"Me, too."

"I'm sorry, Darby." Mandy stared at her hands, took a deep breath and continued. "I had no right to do what I did."

Darby didn't have to ask what she meant. "Why did you?"

"Trey."

"You were the one to dump him," Darby reminded her.

"Because I thought he had feelings for you, and then he asked you to the prom. I..." Mandy's concerned brown eyes lifted to

Darby's. "I was wrong to do what I did, to inter-fere. All I can say in my defense is that I've always loved Trey."

"Yet you ended things with him a second time."

"Not because I didn't love him."

"Then why?"

"Because I couldn't stand that I'd destroyed our friendship over a guy."

Mandy's words sank in.

"What happened on prom night and the week after was poison to my relationship with Trey. I didn't think I deserved to be happy with him, so I refused to be happy." Mandy wrung her hands together, shrugged. "If I hadn't broken up with him when I did he'd have dumped me, which is what I deserved, but I beat him to the punch."

"I always thought you two would end up married," Darby mused. "When I heard he'd taken a job out of town and married someone else I was shocked."

"I cried myself to sleep for weeks." Mandy's hands twisted the thin material of her shirt. "I know it's wrong to be happy when someone's marriage falls apart, but when I heard Trey was divorcing I knew why I'd stayed single all these years." She let out a deep breath. "I was waiting for him. Not because I thought he'd get divorced, but because I didn't want anyone but him. Yet even with him single, I still can't have him."

"Why not?"

"My conscience won't let me."

"Because of what happened with me?" Darby asked in surprise, not quite believing what she was hearing. All these years she'd assumed Mandy hadn't cared how she'd hurt her.

"It wasn't until yesterday at the picnic, when I saw you with Blake, that I knew you and Trey weren't meant to be together."

Had it only been yesterday? The picnic seemed so long ago.

"You and Blake are perfect together."

Perfect?

They'd been perfect last night in bed.

They'd been perfect partners prior to this weekend.

Now? Darby wasn't sure *perfect* was the right adjective for what was happening between her and Blake.

"I envy you." Mandy grimaced. "I have another admission to make. Despite knowing I couldn't be with Trey, I couldn't bring myself to mail your invitation. I wanted you here for so many reasons, yet I was scared of what might happen when you came home." Mandy grasped her arm. "Can you ever forgive me?"

Surprised by all the emotional swings the weekend had brought, Darby glanced at the woman who'd once been her best friend, thought about all that had transpired, and tried to let go of past hurts. "I can forgive you, but I'm not sure I have it in me to do more than that. Too much has happened, too many hurts."

Tears shining in her eyes, Mandy nodded.

"Darby, is everything okay?"

Darby turned, stared at Trey, then beyond him to where Blake stood. Apparently both men had tired of waiting and come in search of them.

Seeing Trey's gaze go beyond her to Mandy, Darby nodded. "Everything's fine."

Except that her mother was lying in a hospital bed fighting for her life and she'd once again fallen for a man who didn't love her.

Darby and Blake watched Mandy and Trey leave. Mandy turned and waved. With a forced smile on her face, Darby waved back.

"What happened between you and Mandy?"

"We aired a few things." She turned to look at Blake, wondering how she could be so aware of him physically even when they stood outside the hospital. "I'm not going back to Knoxville tonight."

"I suspected as much. Do you want me to get us a hotel room here in Pea Ridge?"

Did she? Maybe if they were alone they could talk—could air things between them, too. Like the fact that she loved him and didn't want to go back to things being the way they were.

"That would be great."

"I'll call Dr. Kingston and ask him to cover for us. And I'll get in touch with our office manager and let her know what's going on, so she can reschedule our appointments for tomorrow."

She nodded. "You're sure you don't mind staying another night? You could go home tonight."

"I'm not leaving you to face this alone, Darby."

"Thank you." She didn't point out that she wouldn't be alone, that she'd have her family. Because when she closed her eyes tonight she wanted to be wrapped in his arms, with him purging the awful memories of the day, replacing them with new memories, memories full of hope for a better tomorrow.

But late that night, when they arrived at the hotel, Blake did leave her alone.

Alone in a hotel room, with him in a room across the hallway.

Darby cried herself to sleep.

Darby's mother's procedure went well the following day, and although she had mixed feelings about leaving, Darby knew she and

Blake had to go home. If only long enough for her to pack a few things and drive back down by herself. Blake could cover at the office for however long was needed.

Jim walked them out to the parking lot.

Darby hugged her brother goodbye. "I'll keep my phone on me at all times. If anything changes, anything at all, you'll call?"

He nodded. "I don't know why you're asking me. If something changes you'll know before I do. I saw you give the doctor and nurses specific instructions on calling you."

"I don't feel right about leaving," she said for the dozenth time.

"I know." Jim put his arm around her. "But the doctor says she's going to be fine."

Her brother was right, of course.

She turned to Blake, found him watching her, and battled her conflicting desire to pound him with her fists and to lean against his broad shoulders.

They'd barely said two words to each other all day. He'd been with her all the time, but in the background, on the periphery of her life. Was he foreshadowing what to expect when they returned to Knoxville?

When she'd said her goodbyes to her brother, Darby rested her throbbing head against Blake's passenger seat.

"Hungry?"

She shook her head. Food was the last thing she wanted.

"You've not eaten anything since what little you nibbled at breakfast," he pointed out. "I'm starved."

"You can stop somewhere, but I'm not hungry."

"You need to eat, too."

Her stomach rumbled, reminding her that Blake was right. "Fine. I'll eat."

He pulled into a sandwich shop. They went in and ordered sandwiches, fruit, and drinks. Darby ate more than she'd thought she would, and felt better than she had when they'd arrived at the shop. Her headache had even eased.

If only her heartache would.

* * *

Blake stared straight ahead, as if the oncoming interstate traffic was the most fascinating view in the world.

As if he wasn't aware that Darby had given up trying to make conversation, had given up pretending to be asleep and instead had been intently watching him for the past thirty minutes. Her gaze hadn't budged.

Although he was acutely aware of her, he made no acknowledgement of her stare. To do that would open up more conversation attempts, and at the moment talking with Darby was the last thing he wanted.

What he wanted was to punch something.

He couldn't look at Darby and not want her.

He couldn't want her because then he'd want to act upon that want. And to do that would confuse things even more.

Which was why he'd gotten them separate hotel rooms the night before. Darby was vulnerable because of what had happened with her mother, what had happened between them. He'd had no right to take advantage of that vulnerability a second night.

He liked Knoxville. Having moved so many times during his youth, he hadn't really known what he was missing, but now, having been in the same place for several years, he liked the sense of belonging he'd found. Liked the feeling enough to want to protect the life he'd made for himself.

A home, a job, a partner he depended upon. The good life he'd made for himself had evolved around Darby. They shared the same friends from medical school, shared colleagues, shared a clinic.

If he pursued her sexually, when it ended that life would fall down around him.

His best plan of action was to do as he'd done since yesterday. Act as if their making love had been no big deal, and hope that with time their relationship would smooth back out, that he and Darby could be friends again.

All he had to do was convince himself that sex with Darby had been no big deal.

# CHAPTER NINE

"GOOD morning, Mr. Hill," Darby greeted the thin man lying in his hospital bed, a grumpy expression on his wrinkled face.

"It would be a good Tuesday morning if you'd tell me I can go home."

"Let me see how that leg is doing, then we'll talk."

Talk. As she and Blake hadn't done. The drive home last night had been almost unbearable.

Oh, they'd made occasional small talk, but that had been the extent of their conversation.

What had they done?

Better yet, what were they going to do?

How was she supposed to greet him this morning? As her business partner, or as the man she'd made love to repeatedly on Saturday evening and again on Sunday morning?

For Blake, sex was sex. She knew that. Knew that she had to pretend what had happened between them was no big deal because other-wise she'd lose him forever.

Only she wasn't sure she could.

Too much had happened over the weekend.

Too many old wounds opened. Too many questions raised. Too many new emotions that felt too right.

"Does that look mean I'm not going home?" Mr. Hill asked, pulling Darby back to the present.

"I'm afraid not," she admitted, replacing the wet dressing on his leg ulcer. "At least not for several more days. The good news is that your leg is healing, slowly but surely."

"I can't heal at home?"

Home.

Longing pierced her heart. *Home is where the heart is.* So where was home? Knoxville? Armadillo Lake?

"No, I'm sorry, you can't."

She spent a few more minutes talking to him, then left his hospital room. She'd barely taken two steps into the hallway when Blake came out of a patient's room.

Shock at seeing her registered in his eyes. "I wasn't expecting you to be here this early."

Obviously. Did that mean he'd purposely arrived early, in hopes of not bumping into her? Or was she being paranoid?

"After leaving the office on Friday I figured there's a lot to catch up." Why did her explanation feel stilted?

"Me, too." He glanced away, ran his fingers through his dark hair. "How's your mother?"

"Stronger this morning, according to her doctor. Apparently she's in as big a rush to go home as Mr. Hill."

"Glad to hear she's improving." Not meeting her eyes, he nodded. "Guess I'll see you at the office."

He turned and walked away.

Darby bit the inside of her cheek. After his pretending to love her all weekend, his can't-get-away-fast-enough attitude contrasted starkly.

It hurt.

Hurt that she suspected she'd forever lost the easy camaraderie she and Blake had always shared.

What did he expect? That if he acted normal she'd think the weekend had meant something? She knew it didn't. She knew he was a highly sexed man. After all, she'd benefited from all that experience. Repeatedly.

Then another thought hit her. Had she been so bad that he couldn't even meet her eyes? Surely not, or he wouldn't have made love to her again on Sunday morning? He had been right there with her, every kiss, every touch, and he had wanted her. He couldn't have faked the desperation with which he'd taken her. He'd been driven, wild, as if he were branding her as his own.

Or was that how all men were when a naked woman squirmed on top of them? Maybe it wouldn't have mattered who she was, or how good or bad she'd been, just that he got sexual relief?

She just didn't know, and Blake hadn't wanted to talk to her on the drive home or after they'd gotten to her apartment and he'd helped carry her things inside. He hadn't even come into her apartment—just set her suitcase inside the front door and skedaddled as if he was worried she'd knock him over the head and drag him to her bed if he lingered.

Why had that hurt so much? Why had she cried herself to sleep for a second night in a row?

When she got to the office, she found exactly what she'd expected to find. A desk piled with things for her to do.

Instead of starting the process of clearing the mountain of work she went to Blake's office, and found him diligently making his way through his own mountain.

"Are you upset with me because of what happened between us?"

"No." Clearly surprised by her candid question, he leaned back in his chair. "I'm upset with myself."

"Why?"

"Because we crossed lines we shouldn't have crossed."

Which said it all. Blake regretted what they'd done. Everything he'd done since Sunday morning had said that he did. Which left her with two options: pretend she regretted what had happened or tell him the truth—that she loved him.

"Fine." She shrugged. "We'll forget this weekend ever happened."

Blake's eyes narrowed. "Can we?"

"I already have." She lifted her chin, stared at him defiantly, her breaking heart well hidden beneath the professional veneer she'd perfected years ago. "Haven't you?"

It had been a hell of a morning and this afternoon was promising to be just as trying. Blake's schedule was packed, and he'd had one call after another from the hospital.

But the worst of it was that he couldn't keep his mind on his work. No, any lull and his mind went to wondering about Darby.

She'd forgotten what they'd done?

If only he believed her.

If only he could get the memories of her body arched into his out of his head.

He couldn't.

Last night he hadn't slept, thanks to missing her warm body snuggled next to his. The night before, lying in a strange hotel room, hadn't been any better. He'd never missed a woman before. Not in bed. He'd always preferred sleeping alone. Apparently that no longer held true.

He preferred Darby.

He'd missed the way she smelled—missed it so much he'd gone out to his car to retrieve the pillow she'd accidentally left in his SUV.

When he finally had gone to sleep it had been while holding her damn pillow, surrounded by her scent, dreaming of her eager kisses.

"Dr. Di Angelo?" His nurse caught him as he followed the patient he'd just finished seeing out of the exam room. "I put McKenzie Bartholomew into room four just then. She's having an allergic reaction."

Blake immediately stepped into the room, took one look at his patient's enormous lower lip, and agreed with his nurse's assessment. "What happened?"

"I've no idea. I was outside in our pool and my lips started tingling. A few minutes later my lip started swelling and we headed straight here."

Blake looked over her medication allergies, stuck his head out the door and ordered an injection to be administered.

Taking his stethoscope, he listened to the girl's heart and lungs. Although her heart-rate was slightly increased, at a hundred and four beats a minute, her breathing was normal, with no wheeze.

"My nurse will be in to give you some epinephrine, and I'll be back in to check on you in a few minutes."

He stepped out of the exam room, his gaze colliding with Darby's the second he did so.

"Everything okay?"

"Fine."

"Good."

"Thanks."

Having had enough of the monosyllabic

dialogue, Blake took a deep breath and went into his next patient's room.

A month later, Darby was examining the right arm of an older man with a bad combover. "You're sure you didn't hit your arm?"

The man's hearing wasn't the best, and he stared at her, clearly not comprehending.

"Your arm—did you hit it?" she repeated louder.

He shook his head. "My fingers started hurting first, then the pain moved up my arm. When I took my shirt off last night, this is what I saw."

"This" being the dark purplish discoloration that ran from his shoulder to fade into his palm. The entire underside of his arm looked as if someone had beaten him.

"Have you accidentally taken extra of your blood thinner?"

Again he couldn't understand her, and she repeated her question.

His blood *had* to be overly thin. There could be little other explanation for his unusual symptoms. Still, under normal circumstances she'd have sought out Blake for a second opinion.

This was ridiculous. No matter what had happened last month, they were still partners. Partners who barely spoke, but partners. When they did speak, it was usually Blake asking about her mother, about her trips to Armadillo Lake over the weekends to stay with her family. Occasionally they spoke about patients, but never did they mention what had happened.

Darby kept hoping, kept praying that he'd relax, would realize that what they'd shared had been special. Instead they only seemed to be growing further apart. Each day felt more tense than the one before.

She was tired of it. Tired of walking on egg-shells. Tired of his ignoring her. Tired of feeling like she'd lost her best friend.

She wanted his opinion on a patient, and by golly she was going to get it.

She excused herself and poked her head into the room where Blake had just finished with a patient. "Can I see you for a few minutes?"

She saw his hesitation, saw his eyes narrow before he answered. "What's up?"

"I'd like you to take a look at Clinton Rogers' arm. I suspect his blood is too thin but the results aren't back yet."

"What's going on?"

"No history of injury, but pain in his right arm eight on a scale of ten, that started at the base of his middle finger and moved up his arm. Started yesterday. When he undressed last night his arm was deep purple and felt cold to him."

"Why didn't he go to the emergency room?"

"You tell me." Mr. Rogers should have gone to the ER, but he hadn't. Now it was her job to decide if he needed to be admitted or if he could be treated at home, probably with vitamin K injections, pending his laboratory results.

Blake followed her into the room, examined Mr. Rogers' arm, then spoke loudly to the older man. "I'm going to drain this pocket of blood."

Darby nodded. She'd planned to do the same, but had opted to wait until the laboratory results were back prior to doing so.

Gathering the supplies he'd need out of the exam room drawer, Darby handed Blake a ten milliliter syringe with a large-gauge needle attached. Their fingers brushed, their eyes met. Her breath caught and held.

"Blake?" She couldn't hold back the emotion bubbling inside her. They hadn't touched since that weekend, and instantly Darby was filled with longing, filled with memories of their making love.

His gaze narrowed, grew cold. He turned his back to her, explaining quite loudly to Mr. Rogers what he planned to do.

He'd snubbed her, rejected her all over again.

Darby's hope that things would get better between them died a painful death.

She'd taken a chance the weekend of the reunion, and she'd lost. Lost not only the hope that Blake might someday love her, but lost him from her life completely—because she couldn't stand this hostile environment.

Couldn't stand to breathe the same air. Not when seeing him, smelling his spicy scent, hearing his voice, only served to remind her of what could have been had he only loved her.

She left the room, intending to check on Mr. Rogers' lab results. Instead she found herself dialing Mandy's number.

"Coulson Realty." Mandy had gone to work at her father's real estate company. "Mandy Coulson speaking."

"Mandy, this is Darby Phillips. Is Mack Donahue's place still for sale? I want to make an offer."

The following week, Darby stared at the blue lines on the test.

Pregnant.

How could she be pregnant? She and Blake had used protection. Maybe the test was wrong. Although most accurate with an early-morning sample, she hadn't waited. From the moment she'd realized her period hadn't arrived last week, not knowing had driven her crazy.

No doubt about it. Even with the time of day, and only being a week late, the positive had been strong and almost immediate. Hcg hormone was present in her urine.

The implications caused her head to spin.

Pregnant.

She was having a baby.

There was a baby growing inside her body this very minute.

Her, a mother.

She'd have to schedule an appointment with her gynecologist.

She'd have to tell Blake.

Blake.

They'd made a baby together.

How would he react?

Not well. With each day that passed they grew further apart, making her long for the days of his teasing, making her long for his touch.

She missed him, hadn't realized just how much time she'd spent with Blake until he'd blaringly exited her life.

Oh, he was still physically around. They worked in the same office, did rounds at the same hospital, but he went out of his way to avoid her and, unable to stand the regret in his dark eyes, the wince that often followed his seeing her, she'd taken to avoiding him, too.

Not only that, but she'd signed a contract on the house and five acres of the Mack Donahue estate in Armadillo Lake, and had been trying to decide just what that meant. She missed her family, was desperately needed in Armadillo Lake, but was she really planning to move home? Was she giving up on Blake?

She kept hoping they'd slip back into the easy relationship they'd always shared. After all, time healed all wounds.

Now she knew that was an impossibility.

They'd never go back.

When she told Blake she was pregnant, her news would forever destroy any hope of that.

She missed everything about him—his smile, his teasing, his wit, his friendship, his kisses. Everything.

Still, she had to think about the baby—a baby! His baby. She and Blake would have to talk, would have to figure out how they wanted to handle the future.

For her, abortion wasn't an option. If Blake wanted her to go that route he'd have to think again. He wouldn't suggest terminating her pregnancy, though.

Or maybe he would.

She just didn't know anymore.

Knowing she'd been in the private bathroom she and Blake shared too long already, she picked up the plastic pregnancy kit, clenched the test tightly in her sweaty palm. She couldn't leave the kit. Nor could she leave the wrapper.

Gathering up the test she'd taken from their small lab, she stuffed it into her purse and zipped the oversized bag to hide all evidence.

Planning to lock her purse in her desk drawer, she stepped into the hallway separating her and Blake's offices.

They rarely shut their office doors, so as usual his was open. His voice carried out into the hallway.

"I'll swing by and do rounds before I go home tonight."

Darby's gaze was drawn to where he sat at his desk. His dark head was bent, studying a paper on his desk while he spoke on the phone. Would their baby have his dark eyes and hair? His superb bone structure? His quick wit and smile?

The depth of emotion swamping her stunned her. Never had she considered getting pregnant, but she wanted Blake's baby.

Unaware that she watched him, he initialed the paper, then flipped to the next. "Go ahead and draw another CBC. I'll check the results when I'm there later." He glanced up, saw her. His mouth tightened into a thin line of displeasure.

An intense longing for the days when he would wink or grin or motion for her to come into his office hit Darby.

She was pregnant.

With his baby.

Oh, Blake.

Of their own accord, her hands went to her belly.

His narrowed gaze lowered, widened, then rose to hers, full of wonder and question.

Darby's stomach lurched. He knew.

She had never been good at hiding her emotions. Why would an unexpected pregnancy be the exception? She should have known Blake would take one look at her and know.

Whether or not she was ready to share her news, Blake knew.

They were going to be parents.

# CHAPTER TEN

"I'VE got to go," Blake told the nurse he spoke with, his gaze never moving from Darby's guilty face. "I'll take care of anything else when I'm at the hospital."

An invisible hand kneading his insides, he hung up the phone and stared at the pale woman standing outside his office, watching him with mounting horror.

Was she?

Her mouth opened, almost as if she'd heard his silent question, but no words came out.

No denial. Only her hand lying protectively over her lower abdomen. Which was really the only answer needed.

Oh, hell.

Darby was pregnant.

His legs trembled at the implications of those three little words. Darby was pregnant.

His hands shook.

His stomach twisted.

His brain throbbed.

His heart squeezed.

Darby was pregnant.

Unsure if his legs would work, he pushed out from his desk, held on to the corner for support as he stood.

He was going to be a father.

Him.

He'd always thought that someday he'd marry, have children, pass on his grandfather's name— but now? Never had he had those thoughts in correlation with anytime soon.

"Darby?"

She shook her head, held up her hand to ward him off, almost as if she couldn't catch her breath. Her eyes had widened to tumultuous deep blue seas.

Did she think he'd be angry at her?

Never.

If anything, he was angry at himself. Clearly he'd been the one with the experience. He had no one to blame except himself for their mistake. His eyes dropped to her belly and he winced.

Mistake.

The idea that he'd thought of his child, his baby, as a mistake sucker-punched him.

His grandfather would roll with shame. Nothing was more precious than family.

If Darby was pregnant, he'd accept that fate and embrace the future, embrace the baby they'd made together, and somehow they'd make it work.

"We need to talk."

Her vocal cords apparently not working, she silently nodded, stepped into his office.

Blake shut the door behind her, not wanting their conversation to be overheard by any of their staff.

"You're pregnant." He didn't ask it as a question. Not when he could so clearly read the truth on her face.

Her eyes searching his, she nodded again.

He didn't ask if the baby was his. Didn't ask how far along. He didn't need to.

His thoughts reeling, he sank onto the corner of his desk. "How do you feel about that?"

Her face pinched and she found her voice. "What do you mean, how do I feel about that? I'm floored."

Blake stared at her, wondering if he'd said the wrong thing. Hell, what was the right thing in this situation? Was he supposed to say he'd be there every step of the way with her? That he'd go to Lamaze classes and be in the delivery room? That he'd be an active father in their child's life? Was he supposed to tell her that he was as floored as she was, but that this was their baby they were talking about and, floored or not, he'd be the kind of father he'd never had?

A million thoughts, a million questions, ran through his mind all at once. Questions he didn't have the answers to. The woman who did have those answers stood before him with pink tingeing her cheeks.

"What do you expect of me?" Did she want him to propose? To give their child legitimacy?

She blinked. "Expect of you?"

"What do you want me to do, Darby? Marry you? Agree to support you financially?" Blake's throat tightened, his hands sweated, his heart pounded. "Tell me what you expect of me and how all this makes you feel so I know what I need to do."

Was Blake kidding? Darby stared at the man leaning on his desk and wondered if she'd ever known him at all. Had he really just asked what she *expected* of him? How she felt about being pregnant?

"Nothing." She wished she had something to throw at him. Something hard. And sharp. Her gaze landed on the stress relief ball. That soft little thing wouldn't begin to relieve the stress mounting inside her. Not even if the ball smacked him square between the eyes. "I don't expect anything from you."

"Every woman expects something from the man who's gotten her pregnant."

"You've already done more than enough."

"It's too late to point fingers, Darby. I take full responsibility. I know your baby's mine."

She hadn't even considered that he might think otherwise, so his comment stung even more.

She pressed her fingertip to her throbbing temple, hoping to calm the wild pulse hammering there. "You want to know how I feel? What I expect? I don't know, Blake. I only just did the test, and I don't know how I feel about any of this."

"You missed your period? That's why you did the test?"

Give Sherlock a cookie.

"I'm a week late." She glanced at him, tried not to wince at the tight lines of his face. How could he look so familiar, and yet so alien at the same time? "I kept telling myself stress was causing my missed cycle, but…"

"It wasn't."

She dug in her purse, pulled out the plastic kit

from where she'd slid it inside the wrapper, and handed the confirmation of her suspicions to him.

"No."

Blake studied the plastic wand with eyes darker than she recalled ever seeing them. So dark they paled the night sky.

"You're pregnant."

Yes, they'd already established that.

Her legs growing weak beneath her, she sat down on the edge of his desk, next to him.

"I'm pregnant."

The rest of Blake's evening passed in a blur.

No wonder.

He was going to be a father.

How had that happened?

He knew *how* that had happened, just… Blake knocked on Darby's front door, wishing she'd hurry and let him into the apartment she'd lived in since they were in medical school.

An apartment that wouldn't be big enough for her and a baby.

She'd need more space—a place with a yard big enough for a swing and a sandbox.

When she opened the door, his heart lurched at her red-rimmed, swollen eyes. All day he'd been caught up in his own feelings about Darby's news. He'd asked how she felt, but truth was he'd asked in regard to how her feelings affected *him*.

How could he have been so callous?

"You've been crying."

Emitting a low sniffle, she rolled her puffy eyes at him. "So? Pregnant women cry."

He supposed they did.

"Are you going to invite me in?"

Sighing, she stepped back, waited for him to enter the apartment, then shut the door.

He sat down on her living room sofa, looking around for something to focus on besides the woman he wanted to take into his arms and promise it would all be all right. Somehow.

"You said you wanted to come by so we could talk," she reminded him. "I don't know what to say, Blake, so you're going to have to do the talking."

He didn't know where to start.

"I'm sorry I put you in this position."

She didn't glance at him, just sank onto an overstuffed chair at the far end of the sofa and curled her legs beneath her. "You weren't the only one in that hotel room. My getting pregnant took both of us."

That it had. Blake vividly recalled just what the two of them had done to get her pregnant, was haunted by the memories every time he closed his eyes, every time he saw her.

"We can't change the past."

"No," he agreed, wondering when talking to Darby had gotten so difficult, when he'd gotten self-conscious of each word. Of course he knew the precise moment. When they'd become lovers. He ached for his easy relationship with Darby, ached for what he'd lost in her friendship, her partnership. But she was right. They couldn't change the past. "Which leaves us trying to make the best of the future."

Her head lowered to her hands. "Agreed."

"I know you got upset when I asked this

earlier, but my question was a legitimate one."
He moved to the end of the sofa closest to her,
reached for her hand, but she jerked away,
shaking her head rapidly back and forth.

Trying to convince himself that Darby's rejection wasn't the cause of the sharp pain slashing
across his chest, Blake sighed. "Tell me what
you want, Darby?"

What *did* she want? Darby wondered.

"I want us to go back to the way we were," she
admitted, surprised at her candor, but figuring
at this point she had nothing to lose. She'd
already lost the best thing in her life, the thing
she'd had for years yet hadn't had at all—him.
"I miss my partner and friend."

He nodded as if he understood. "I've missed
you, too."

He had? "Have you? I haven't gotten that im-
pression these past few weeks."

"Our friendship and business relationship was
special to me. I hate that we let sex come
between that."

Friendship. Business relationship. Sex.

Darby winced.

"Our relationship won't ever be the same, Darby. No matter how hard we try, we can't go back to how things were."

Perhaps she'd said the wrong thing. Because she really didn't want what they'd had before. She wanted what she'd had in Alabama. She wanted Blake to be in love with her. For real.

She wanted to look into his eyes and see desire and love for her.

She wanted him to feel the same about her as she felt about him.

Because she was in love with Blake.

"I don't want to go back to how things were."

His brow arched. "You don't? But didn't you just say…?"

She shook her head. "I thought that was what I wanted, but I want more."

Eyes narrowed, Blake worked his throat, gulped. "More?"

So much had happened in the past few hours that it probably wasn't wise to make grand life decisions, but Darby did. In her heart she knew she was making the right choice.

"I want to sell my half of the clinic to you, Blake. I'm going home."

"No." Steely determination shone in his eyes.

Darby frowned. "What do you mean, no? No, you don't want to buy my half of the clinic?" She shrugged. "Fine. I'll find another doctor to buy my half out. Our business contract reads that we have to offer each other first option, so that's what I was doing."

"I'm not buying your half of the clinic because you aren't selling." His tone brooked no argument.

Not quite believing his reaction, Darby stared at him, more determined than ever that she was making the right choice for her and the baby. "Actually, I am. I'm going home."

"Knoxville is your home."

"No," she sighed. "It's not. I belong in Armadillo Lake. They need a doctor."

"You don't belong there. You blackmailed me into going to your high school reunion so you wouldn't have to go there alone."

"I was an immature young girl who held on to her hurt way too long and let those hurts influence life decisions in ways I shouldn't have."

"What about me?"

He'd been the main reason she'd stayed in Knoxville. She'd wanted to be near him. Still, there was more to think about than her or Blake. She had to consider what was right for their baby.

"What about you?"

Good question. One Blake didn't have an answer to. He didn't have answers to anything. Just knew that he didn't want Darby to leave Knoxville.

Didn't want her to leave him.

She might not feel she belonged here, but Blake did. For the first time in his life he belonged somewhere, truly felt at home.

Darby couldn't just rip that feeling all to pieces. He wouldn't let her.

"I have rights, too, you know."

Her forehead wrinkled. "Rights?"

"Regarding your pregnancy. Moving doesn't

just affect you. Where you live affects me and my relationship with our child."

Darby's mouth dropped. "I wouldn't stop you from seeing our baby. You should know that, Blake."

"Should I?" Pain at the thought of his world being ripped apart clouded his judgement and he lashed out. "How do I know you aren't moving home to pick things up with Nix? That you aren't hoping he'll step in and play house with you and my baby? Is that what you've been doing in Alabama while I've covered your patients? Did you see him?"

Darby blinked. "You're kidding, right?"

"No."

"I have talked to Trey since that weekend, but not in the manner you're implying."

"Since the weekend you became pregnant with my baby, you mean?"

She gave him a stubborn look. "Yes, the weekend of the reunion."

"And Mandy? Have you talked to her?"

"Yes."

"And?"

"We've made our peace. You know that. You were at the hospital that afternoon, with her and Trey."

"Yes, I was," he snarled.

She stared at him. "What is wrong with you? Trey and Mandy are dating again. I'm happy for them. Their being together is how it should have been all along." She frowned. "If I didn't know better, I'd think you were jealous."

"Good thing you do know better."

"Yes, it is." She shook her head. "I don't want to argue with you, but I *am* going to sell my half of the clinic. If you want to buy me out, fine. If not, I'd love to say I'll just walk away, but I'll need the funds to start my life in Alabama."

Funds? She really had no idea as to his wealth, did she? Wealth any child of Blake's would be entitled to. Darby would never have to work another day if she chose not to.

"You're really going to leave me? On the day you discover you're pregnant with my baby, you're announcing you want me to buy your half of our life together so you can move six hours away?"

She didn't wince, didn't show the slightest remorse, just held his gaze. "I am."

"You believe that's fair to me?"

"I have to think about what's best for me and for our baby. My going home to Armadillo Lake is what's best."

"Why?"

"Because my family is there, and it's where I was meant to be. I'd forgotten that for a while, but a memory lapse doesn't make the truth any less true."

"You were meant to be with me."

At her surprised look, he added, "In Knoxville, at our clinic. We have a good thing, Darby. A good practice."

"It hasn't been good since we slept together, and you know it. You can barely tolerate looking at me."

"That's not true."

"It is," she accused, standing up from her chair and pacing across her living room. She spun toward him, her eyes as accusing as her tone. "You've been avoiding me ever since we slept together, and I can't stand it."

"That's why you want to move? To punish me for sleeping with you?"

"That's not what I said, Blake. I don't want to punish you. I just can't deal with the way things are between us now."

"Because we ruined everything when we had sex?"

"Apparently so." She folded her arms across her chest. "It certainly hasn't made things better between us."

No, that weekend had caused the foundation of their relationship to crumble, and now his world was crashing around him.

"What is it you want between us, Darby? What is it you expected after that weekend?"

"I told you, Blake, I don't expect anything from you."

"Apparently you do—or at least you did. Otherwise you wouldn't be leaving me." As he said the words out loud, their validity reverberated through him. She had expected something from him, something he'd failed to deliver.

"You're twisting my words. I'm not leaving *you*."

"How can you say that? You're walking away from everything we have together."

"Not everything, Blake." She placed her hand over her belly. "There's one thing we have together that I won't ever walk away from. You can count on it."

His gaze dropped to her belly and the blood drained from his face. Darby was going to have his baby, but she didn't want him in her life, didn't want to be a family with him.

And then it hit him. Darby had taken him to Armadillo Lake prepared to have sex. She'd had new lingerie, a full box of condoms. Perhaps she'd already gotten what she wanted from him?

"Did you get pregnant on purpose?"

"What? How can you say that? We used condoms."

"Some of them *you* bought. Did you tamper with them?"

Her eyes widened with a mixture of disbelief and anger. "Are you serious? Why would I do that?"

Hurt at her rejection of him egged him on. "No doubt a lot of women would like to reap the benefits of having my baby."

Her eyes flashed with anger. "You arrogant son of a—"

"Fine. I know you didn't get pregnant intentionally." Blake had had enough. He'd known sleeping with Darby had been a mistake, but he hadn't been able to stop himself. Now she wanted to cut him out of her life. "If you want to leave, I'll make it simple. Have a contract drawn up for your half of the clinic and I'll sign it. You want to take my baby far away from me—fine. I won't stop you. But expect to hear from my lawyer, because I *will* play a role in my child's life."

# CHAPTER ELEVEN

DARBY placed the last of her books into the packing crate. She couldn't believe how quickly the past month had gone by. Yet with the anger and hurt between her and Blake, each minute had also dragged by.

True to his word, he had signed the contract her lawyer had drawn up. She was no longer a partner in their clinic. She was no longer anything to him.

No, not true. She was the mother of his unborn child.

They'd always have that connection. Always.

A tear ran down her cheek.

Although moving home was the right thing for so many reasons, leaving Knoxville wasn't easy. When the movers had crated up the contents of her apartment that morning she'd burst into tears. She'd cried until her chest throbbed. She'd left to finish at the office, because she hadn't been able to watch them empty her apartment.

Because her heart had been breaking.

*Home is where the heart is.*

Her heart was with Blake.

If he'd loved her she would have stayed in Knoxville forever, would have gone wherever he was and been happy.

But he didn't love her.

As she had no choice, she accepted that. But if making him love her were possible, she'd fight for Blake's heart to her dying breath.

For all eternity.

"I can't believe you're really going."

Darby's gaze shot to the doorway. "Blake."

She swiped at her eyes, hoping he hadn't caught the waterworks. "How long have you been standing there?"

Had he come to start yet another fight with her? It seemed as if that was all they did on the few occasions they actually spoke.

God, he looked good, in his black pants and crisp white polo. Then again, when *didn't* he look good?

"Long enough to think you're not as confident about this move as you've let on. It's not too late to change your mind."

She took a deep breath, steeling herself for his verbal attack. "Being sad at saying goodbye doesn't make me any less confident that I've made the right decision."

He pushed off the doorframe, stepped into the office, and closed the door behind him.

Darby swallowed. She wasn't sure she was strong enough to deal with another fight between them. Not now, in her last minutes at the clinic.

"I don't want you to go, Darby."

If she'd thought she wasn't strong enough for an argument, she certainly wasn't strong enough to deal with his soft admission.

She took a step back. "We've been through this."

"But perhaps we haven't said the right things."

Hope lifted high in her chest. "What right things?"

If he asked her to stay, to be a family, told her he loved her, she'd throw her arms around him and stay forever.

"You're a part of my life, Darby. A good part that I don't want to let go."

"Blake, two months have gone by and you've barely acknowledged my existence." Two months in which her heart had broken at every wayward glance, at every smile not returned.

"I've been aware of you every moment of every day. How could I not be?" he asked, moving closer. "You're carrying my child."

The baby. That was why he was here. Why he was looking at her with such longing. Question was, what motivated him? Actual concern for their child, or guilt that he was washing his hands of her and their baby?

"Regardless of where I am, I'll still be carrying your child, Blake. Location doesn't change that."

His lips pursed with displeasure. "Location changes everything."

Location wouldn't change her feelings for

him, but perhaps not having to see him on a daily basis would make dealing with the shattered pieces of her heart slightly easier.

She doubted it, though.

"You know where to find me, Blake." She quit backing up, faced him. "You've always known where to find me. You've just never cared to look. Not at me. Not really."

Inches separated their bodies. He towered over her. "What's that supposed to mean?"

"I've always been right here, Blake."

"Just as I've always been here for you, Darby. Always. Every time you've needed me, I've been here for you."

"You have." She swallowed the knot in her throat. What was he doing?

"Yet you feel the need to leave? To just forget about us?"

She couldn't stand anymore. "Don't you get it, Blake? There has never been an us." She put her palms against his chest. "All we had was one weekend of pretense."

"Is that what you believe?"

"Tell me I'm wrong."

"You're wrong." As if to prove his point, he lowered his mouth to hers, kissed her so thoroughly her knees wobbled. "Tell me you don't feel that, Darby. Tell me you don't want me even now."

"That's only sexual attraction." *Tell me I'm wrong. Please, Blake, tell me you feel more for me than sexual attraction.*

"Don't knock chemistry. It's what makes the world go around."

"Not my world," she admitted softly.

Knowing she had to go while she still could, Darby pulled free from his loose hold.

She'd hoped he'd stop her, that he'd hold on to her and tell her what he felt for her was so much more than sexual attraction.

"If you stay, I'll marry you."

"Why?" *Tell me you love me. I'll go anywhere with you, Blake. Just love me.*

"For the baby."

A part of Darby died. The part that had been holding out hope that maybe, just maybe, he cared for her. But when push came to shove

Blake wouldn't fight for her. Why would he? He didn't love her, and had never given her reason to think he did. In the long run, her leaving made things easier for him.

Darby touched his cheek, loving the feel of the light razor stubble that had popped up since he'd shaved that morning, wishing she could touch him forever.

"Don't make doing the right thing more difficult than it already is, Blake." She stood on her tiptoes, pressed a kiss to his lips, and stepped away. Her gaze landed on the one thing she hadn't yet packed. The one thing she hadn't been able to place inside a packing crate. Her heart.

Picking up the plastic model at its base, she felt memories assail her. Memories all made with Blake. She turned, smiled through her tears, and held out the heart.

"Here," she whispered. "Take this. It seems my heart won't be making the move with me. It's always belonged to you, anyway."

\* \* \*

"What happened to that pretty female doctor?"

Blake frowned at Mr. Hill, and not because of the ulcer on his leg. Fortunately, the ulcer on Mr. Hill's leg now had pink granulation tissue forming and was slowly healing.

"She left."

The man cracked his arthritic neck, frowning right back at Blake. "To be a doctor, she wasn't too bad. Easy on the eye, too. Where'd she go?"

He didn't need a man in his seventies telling him Darby was easy on the eye. Blake knew she was easy on the eye. Good thing too, because whether his eyes were open or closed Darby was always what he saw.

"She moved back to where she came from." Did he sound bitter? Likely. He felt bitter. Darby had found out she was pregnant and immediately left him. Sure, he didn't know much about being a family, but she hadn't even given him a chance.

"Where's that?" Mr. Hill asked.

"Alabama." Blake answered.

Mr. Hill's bushy white brow quirked. "You don't like Alabama?"

"It's a state."

"And misery is a state of mind." Mr. Hill waved his hand in dismissal. "Why are you still here? You should go after her."

"No one asked for your opinion."

"You should have asked. I've been around awhile, learned from life experiences. You should try it sometime."

"I've learned from life experiences." He'd learned that he shouldn't rely on anyone except himself. He'd learned that he'd been a fool to stay in Knoxville following graduation. He should have left, joined a traveling medical group where he could change locales every few months. Wasn't that what he knew best? How not to get close to people because they came and went from your life?

"You ain't learned jack, or you'd be rubbing her leg instead of mine."

Blake dropped his hand away from Mr. Hill's calf. He'd say the older man had a point—

except his rubbing had been covering the wet dressing with an elastic wrap to protect Mr. Hill's clothes from getting stained.

"You don't know what you're talking about."

"I know if I had a pretty young woman's heart I'd be with her."

He didn't have Darby's heart.

Well, actually, he did, but that was just plastic.

Blake froze. Darby's words hit him, pinging through his thick skull and sinking home.

Darby had given him her heart, had said her heart belonged to him.

After a lifetime of abstinence, she had given him her virginity.

She loved him.

He'd been too blind to realize.

Too blind to see.

But how could he have seen when he'd been too blind to even see his own feelings for Darby?

While in Alabama, pretending to love her, he'd realized he wanted her, that he'd always wanted her, but instead of acting upon that re-alization he'd run scared, wanting to hold on to the safe rather than risk getting hurt. To hang on to the tried and true rather than venture into unknown territories. In the process he'd lost her.

Blake set down his stethoscope, stared at Mr. Hill, and gave credit where credit was due. "You're a wise man, Nathan Hill."

The man smiled his toothless smile. "Looks like you're wisening up, too."

"That I am. Let's hope I'm not too late."


"I just can't believe you're really home." Rosy waved her paintbrush, droplets of paint splattering onto the plastic lining the floor. Her gaze lowered to the paint. "Oops."

Darby wiped the back of her hand across her sweaty brow, a smile on her paint-dappled face. Part of her couldn't believe she was home either.

"I can't believe you didn't bring that scrumptious doctor with you," Mandy said, glancing up from where she'd taped off a corner of the room they were painting.

The room where Darby would soon be seeing patients.

In Alabama.

In her own practice.

Far away from the scrumptious doctor in question.

"Blake is busy finding someone to replace me in Knoxville."

Mandy's gaze met Darby's, then lowered to the painter's tape. Darby hated her friend's sympathy. They'd all commiserated when she'd told them she and Blake had broken up. If not for her pregnancy, she would have told them the entire weekend had been nothing more than a pretense.

"In the office or in his bed?" Rosy eyed Darby curiously. "Because, as much as I want you home, I want you to be happy, too, and he made you happy." She gave a considering look. "Understandably so. Just looking at him made me happy, too."

"Whatever." Darby shook her head at Rosy. Her sister-in-law was as in love with her husband as the day they'd exchanged vows. Still, Rosy had a point. "I am happy."

Mandy glanced up at her, eyeing her even more curiously than Rosy had. "You're sure?"

Did her friends think she was depressed? Was that why they visited so often? Mandy had even fussed over Darby's lack of kempt hair and make-up that morning. What did her appearance matter for painting? But she appreciated their concern, so she forced a smile to her face. "I'm sure."

It was the truth. Mostly.

Sure, she cried herself to sleep at night, missing Blake, but she was happy, was confident she'd made the right decision to move home and raise her baby surrounded by her family's love.

She hadn't told anyone of her pregnancy yet. As she was only a little over three months along, she had a while before she had to tell anyone. She wasn't ready. She'd shared enough changes with her family over the past few weeks.

No doubt they would be disappointed that she'd be a single mother. But they'd love her and support her in the months leading up to and following the baby's arrival.

Other than missing Blake, her biggest concern regarding her pregnancy and the move was that the closest OB/GYN was thirty miles away. Still, that shouldn't present a problem, since most first deliveries didn't go quickly, and if it did there was always the calving barn.

As far as Blake replacing her, in the office and in his bed, well, she did her best not to think about that, as the thought of him with another woman hurt deeper than she wanted to admit.

So she'd focused on her new life. All she had to do was finish up the repairs and she'd be ready to open on October first, as planned.

She glanced out the window, catching sight of her brothers, Mark the vet, and Trey, down near the lake. Over the past few weeks, as their time had allowed, while she, Mandy and her sisters-in-law had worked on the inside of the house, the men had cleaned the yard, replaced the roof's shingles, and painted the outside of the house. Now they were building her a new dock.

Just as Darby and Mandy were slowly re-building their friendship, Mandy and Trey were rekindling old flames. Darby couldn't be happier for them.

"Hey, is that Blake with the guys?"

At Rosy's question, Darby's heart slammed into her throat and tried to pound its way out. Surely she was hallucinating. No way was Blake walking toward the house with Trey, Mark, and her brothers. No way.

But he was.

"Apparently, he's not so busy in Knoxville that he can't drop by for a visit," Rosy snickered, giving Darby a knowing smile. "After all, it's only six hours' drive out of his way."

Darby barely glanced her sister-in-law's way, barely took in Mandy's silence and inability to meet her eyes—had her friend *known* Blake was here? She reached up to check her appearance, realized she'd probably only managed to smear paint into her hair.

What was he doing here?

Why hadn't he called first? Surely he should have called prior to making that drive? What if she hadn't been home? What if she'd decided to go to Knoxville? Maybe Mandy really had known he'd be stopping by today.

Which would explain why her friend had fussed about her appearance earlier.

Darby felt light-headed and not from the non-toxic paint fumes or her pregnancy. All oxygen had disappeared the moment Blake stepped into the room.

His black gaze met hers, drank in the sight of her, and she had a flashback to how it had been between them the last time they'd been in Alabama. He'd held her, touched her, kissed her, loved her.

Only he'd been faking. So why was he here now?

Why was he looking at her as if he'd missed her?

As if he wanted to take her in his arms and kiss her until they were both breathless?

Blake wanted to take Darby into his arms and kiss her until they were both breathless, until they could only cling to each other and never let go.

Because he didn't want to let her go. Not ever.

He was probably a fool, but here he was all the same.

In Alabama. His new home.

Not that he technically had a home. Not anymore.

Land, yes—thanks to the real estate Mandy had helped him purchase. Home, no.

But, looking at Darby, he knew he was a hell of a lot closer to home than he'd be anywhere else in the world.

"Blake?" She stepped toward him, realized every eye in the room was watching them, and paused. "What are you doing here?"

"You told me I could visit any time I was in the neighborhood." Was she upset he was here?

"You were in the neighborhood?"

"Actually…" he began, wondering how she was going to react to his news, wondering if she'd think he'd overstepped. Maybe he *had* overstepped? His mother had certainly thought he was crazy when he'd told her of his plans. She'd also wished him luck and been excited at the prospect of being a grandmother, which had surprised him. "Actually, I'm your closest neighbor."

Darby's mouth opened, and she gawked at him as if he were crazy, too. "You are?"

The whole Phillips clan and her friends glared at him. Apparently Darby's less than enthusiastic greeting had clued them in that all was not well in paradise.

"I bought the place next to yours. The land was originally part of this place, but was subdivided into a separate parcel when you bought the house."

Why was he telling her that? Of course she knew the land had been subdivided. God, he was nervous.

"You bought the rest of my land?"

He nodded, noting she'd called the land hers, hoping before all was said and done she'd call *him* hers, too.

Her eyes shone blue as the cloudless sky, piercing him with regrets that he'd let her walk away from him. "Why?"

"Um, I think it's time for us to head home," Rosy said, linking her elbow with her husband's and giving the others in the room a look that said for them to leave, too.

Darby turned, stared blankly at her sister-in-law and the others in the room. Clearly she'd forgotten they weren't alone.

"Me, too," Mandy said, walking over and giving Darby a quick hug. "Call me later to let me know what time you want me to come over and help finish this up. Bye, Blake. Trey, you ready?"

Mandy and Trey left. But, despite their womenfolk tugging on their arms, Darby's brothers didn't budge—just glared at Blake.

Did they know Darby was pregnant with his baby?

They'd been friendly enough outside, but that had been before Darby's obvious surprise at seeing him. They'd thought she'd been expecting him. What had she told her family?

Did they all know what an idiot he'd been? That he'd let her leave Knoxville without telling her how he felt? That he'd let her leave without fighting for her—even after she'd given him her heart?

Literally.

Darby didn't move, and neither did her brothers.

Blake met each of her brothers' gazes, then hers. "Is there somewhere we can talk in private?"

Glaring, Jim crossed his arms. "Nothing you have to say to my sister that you can't say to us."

"It's okay, guys," Darby said, stepping forward and waving them off. "Y'all go on home. I'll be by Mom and Dad's later for dinner. I'll see you there."

"We finished the deck—was just coming in to get you to inspect it," Ralph said, his gaze not leaving Blake.

Darby nodded. "I'll walk out with you guys and take a quick look before y'all leave." She glanced toward Blake, her expression unreadable. "Blake can wait here."

He watched through the large window as she walked to the boat dock with her family, noting that her brothers glanced back toward the house repeatedly, and that Rosy kept a tight hold on her husband's arm.

When the group finally left, Darby didn't

come back inside. Instead she sat down on the dock. With her arms wrapped around her legs, her chin resting on her knees, she stared out at the lake as if the weight of the world was upon her.

Blake figured he was that weight.

What was Blake doing here? What did it mean that he'd bought the rest of the Donahue estate? She'd known he had some family money, but surely not enough to afford all that property connected to the lake and her place? The price had been astronomical.

What did she want his buying the rest of her land to mean?

Ha, that was a trick question.

She wanted it to mean he loved her and had come to sweep her off her feet and marry her.

But if he proposed, did that really mean he loved her? Or just that he'd been hit by a wave of guilt, or responsibility or whatever, and wanted to give their baby a home? A family?

Even if he looked at her with love, she wouldn't

really know. After all, she'd seen what a great actor he was on the weekend of the reunion.

If Blake wanted her to believe he loved her, that was what she'd believe.

But would she really?

Did she really want to be with a man when she wasn't sure why he was with her? A man she loved whole-heartedly but who didn't love her in return? But what about their baby? Didn't she owe it to their baby to give him the benefit of the doubt?

Oh, this was crazy. If she wanted to know why Blake was here, what was she doing outside? Why wasn't she inside, *asking* him why he was here? Why he'd bought the rest of her dream property?

She started to push herself up from the dock, but realized Blake stood behind her. How long had he been there?

"You didn't come back inside," he said softly, moving onto the deck and sitting down beside her. He sat close enough that she felt his body heat, close enough that she could breathe in his musky scent. Close enough that she wanted to lean against his shoulder, feel his arms around her, and stay there forever.

Instead, she continued to look out at the lake, pretending to be mesmerized by the sunshine bouncing off the water.

"I needed a few minutes to digest that you're here." She could feel his gaze on her, wanted to turn and look at him, but refused.

"Is my being here a bad thing?" he asked.

"Just unexpected. You're always welcome, Blake. I told you that. I won't try to keep you away from the baby." Unable not to, she glanced toward him. "Is that why you bought the land next to mine? So you could build a place to stay when you come to visit our child?"

He blew out a long breath and shook his head. "I sold everything in Knoxville."

Her head jerked up. "You did what?"

"I sold the practice to Dr. Kingston, my house to an out-of-state couple. I'm moving to Armadillo Lake permanently."

"But…but what will you do?"

"I've applied for an Alabama medical license. I plan to practice here."

"But…but why?"

"Simple." His gaze met hers, held. "You're here."

"And the baby?"

"Yes, and our baby." He glanced toward her flat belly. "How are you feeling? Any morning sickness?"

"Mild nausea, but that's it." She studied him, wondering if she'd inhaled too many paint fumes and was imagining that he was really here. Maybe she'd fainted and was lying on the floor of her future examination room. "You really sold out in Knoxville?"

"I did."

"But you liked Knoxville."

"Not after you left."

Darby's heart came to a quick halt. What was he saying? Had he been struck by guilt that she'd taken off pregnant and alone? Had he felt responsible? Felt he had to come to Alabama to take care of her and their baby?

"Tell me you want me here, Darby. Tell me I'm welcome in your life still."

"I want you here." More than anything she wanted him with her. Always. But not because they were business partners. She wanted Blake in her life because he couldn't imagine his life without her. "You're welcome in my life."

His gaze searched hers. "Tell me you've missed me as much as I've missed you."

"Okay." She nodded, wondering where he was going with this, wondering why her heart shook like a motor sputtering to life. "I've missed you as much as you've missed me." More. Lots more, she silently added.

"This seems to be working pretty well." He took her hand into his, traced over the lines on her palm, then laced their fingers and gave a tight squeeze. "Let's try another. Tell me you love me as much as I love you."

Darby wanted to believe him. Really she did. After all, his eyes shone with sincerity. His palm felt clammy next to hers, as if he was nervous as he waited for her answer.

She sighed, pulled her hand from his. "You know how I feel about you, Blake."

"Do I?"

"I told you."

"What exactly did you tell me, Darby?"

"That my heart has always belonged to you."

"And then you gave me that plastic model heart." He shook his head. "I was stupid, Darby. Utterly stupid. I thought you meant the model, but you didn't, did you?"

Panic seized her, making her feel the need to protect herself. "I did give you the model, Blake."

"But you'd given me your heart a long time before that, hadn't you? That's why you stayed in Knoxville to begin with? Because I was there?"

She rolled her eyes at him, turned to look out over the lake. "You're so conceited."

"Tell me I'm wrong."

"You're wrong."

"You're lying."

Through her teeth.

"Maybe," she conceded.

"I stayed in Knoxville because of you, too,

Darby. I stayed because I wanted to be with you even before I knew that was what I wanted."

Her head jerked toward him. "Huh?"

"Even though you and I weren't a couple, I felt closer to you than to any woman I'd ever known. When I was with you I felt as if I belonged, as if I'd come home. I wasn't ready to acknowledge the attraction I felt for you, because quite frankly you scared the hell out of me, but I wasn't ready to walk away from you either."

"You let me walk away."

"I was an idiot."

Emotions doing jumping jacks inside her chest, Darby leaned her head against her knees, stared out at the water, scared to believe him. "So where does this leave us?"

"It leaves me madly in love with the woman I've come to convince to give me a second chance."

"Blake, you don't have to say things like this just because I'm pregnant."

"I'm not saying anything I don't fully believe."

"You believe you're in love with me?"

"I am in love with you."

She shook her head, thinking this was too much to take in. "You're just in shock from the changes at work. From the fact that I walked away from our business. From the fact that our weekend together resulted in my getting pregnant. That's all this is about, Blake. You miss practicing with me."

"I do miss practicing with you, but there are certainly things I miss more about you than our working together."

"Like?" she couldn't resist asking.

"Like how you smile at me when I walk into a room. How when something perplexes you, you ask my opinion and really listen to my answer. How when my lips touch yours my entire body catches on fire."

She liked all those same things about Blake. He'd always believed in her, always been confident in her abilities, and his confidence in her had given her strength.

"Your body catches on fire when we kiss?"

He studied her. "Yours doesn't?"

She nodded. "Yes, my body catches on fire

when you kiss me, but that doesn't explain why you're here."

"To convince you to let me be your partner in Alabama, Darby. With the baby, you're going to need my help."

With the baby.

Was that why he was saying all the right things? Because he'd resigned himself to a life with her because he'd gotten her pregnant? "I'll get by."

"You'd get by easier with a partner," he pointed out. "I have references. I'm sure my last partner would be willing to put in a good word for me."

"Ha-ha, too funny."

"I'm being serious, Darby." He lifted her hand to his lips, pressed a kiss to her fingertips. "I want to be a part of your life. I've never considered living in Alabama, but I do know I belong wherever you are."

Darby's heart filled with love, filled with the knowledge that Blake loved her. Not because she was pregnant, but because he hadn't been pretending that weekend any more than she had. "How do you know?"

"Because home is where the heart is, and my heart is wherever you are."

# EPILOGUE

WHEN Darby and Blake had added the fully equipped birthing room, they hadn't intentionally meant to be the first couple to make use of its facilities.

"You're sure you're okay?" Blake asked at the end of her latest contraction. He moved from where he'd been between her legs, pressed a kiss to her temple.

. She smiled at her worried husband. Playing the role of both expectant father and doctor perhaps hadn't been their wisest choice. But Darby wouldn't have chosen any other way. Together they'd made their precious baby, and together they would bring him into the world. Just the two of them.

Of course the moment her family realized they

weren't going to show for Sunday dinner, the entire crew would no doubt descend upon them.

"I'm fine."

At the moment she really was. If he asked her after the next contraction started she'd likely tell him otherwise, though. Not that he didn't know. Her last contraction had almost had her head spinning backwards and her cursing his manhood.

Which would be a real shame, since she'd developed quite an attachment to everything about her husband.

Each morning when she woke curled next to him, looked into his happy black eyes first thing, she wanted to pinch herself. Never had she imagined she could be so happy, so loved.

Blake loved her. With all his heart and soul.

When he'd slid the golden band on her ring finger last September, while standing on the dock with their family and friends on the bank, he'd said his vows to her. Love much brighter than the sunshine on the lake had shone in his eyes. Love real and wonderful and all-consuming.

The skin on her belly began pulling tight,

warning the next contraction was starting. They were getting close. So very close to welcoming their baby into the world.

"Maybe we should have driven to Pea Ridge."

Darby shook her head. For as long as she could remember she'd loved this house, had dreamed of someday owning it. Over the past few months she and Blake had made the house their home, taking pride in each room, taking pleasure in decorating the nursery just off their bedroom. Giving birth to their son here would just ice the dream cake.

Or so she'd thought, since she'd wanted to deliver naturally anyway.

As the pressure low in her abdomen continued to build, she admitted she was now seeing the attraction of an epidural.

Her stomach clenched. Sweat beaded on her forehead.

Blake glanced from the monitor strip to Darby's gritted teeth. "Breathe."

Unable to speak, she nodded, the intense pain ripping her body almost unbearable.

"Push, Darby. He's almost here."

Surely she'd die any moment from the pain?

"One more push."

Darby pushed. And pushed.

Blake's cry of awe, followed by another cry, was her reward.

"He's beautiful, Darby."

Darby's gaze went to her red-faced son, lying on her belly. Blake cut and clamped the cord, wrapped their son in a soft cotton blanket, and handed him to Darby's waiting arms.

"He's perfect, Darby. Just like you."

Darby was too wowed by the precious bundle in her arms to laugh at Blake's "Just like you." Someday soon she'd remind him of her "perfection", but for the moment she could only stare at their baby. Jet-black hair covered his round little head. Ten fingers. Ten toes. The sweetest bow-shaped mouth. Perfect.

"Victor Charles Di Angelo." Darby said her son's name out loud, holding the baby where Blake could see him, too.

"It's not too late to name him Dillon."

"Never." She faked a shudder, knowing how

pleased Blake had been at her suggestion of naming their son after his grandfather and her father.

"Don't say I didn't offer." He winked, love shining in his eyes.

"I won't," she promised. "You've been offering for the past six months, despite my repeatedly telling you we aren't naming our son after a high school mascot."

Her gaze dropped back to the yawning baby in her arms. She couldn't resist touching his cheek, running the pad of her fingertip over the smooth softness. His unfocused dark blue eyes stared at her, stealing her heart.

"Welcome to your new home, darling."

"He probably liked his old home better," Blake teased, bending to kiss Darby's cheek. "I know I certainly would."

Darby shook her head. "You're crazy, City Boy."

"About you. Maybe Victor needs a baby brother."

Meeting his gaze, she smiled, knowing where he was going with this. "Named Dillon?"

Grinning, he nodded.

Darby laughed, happier than she could ever remember being. Well, except for perhaps on her wedding day. Her wedding night. And quite a few days and nights since.

She laughed again. "I love you."

"I love you, too, Darby. With all my heart." He kissed her, then placed his hand over where the baby's fist wrapped around her finger. "Thank you."

She didn't have to ask what for. She knew. Knew, and was thankful to Blake for the same things. Remembering what he'd told her that afternoon on the dock, she couldn't agree more.

Home was where the heart was—and she'd come home to stay, for her own happily-ever-after.

# MEDICAL™

## Large Print

*Titles for the next six months…*

### *December*

| | |
|---|---|
| THE MIDWIFE AND THE MILLIONAIRE | Fiona McArthur |
| FROM SINGLE MUM TO LADY | Judy Campbell |
| KNIGHT ON THE CHILDREN'S WARD | Carol Marinelli |
| CHILDREN'S DOCTOR, SHY NURSE | Molly Evans |
| HAWAIIAN SUNSET, DREAM PROPOSAL | Joanna Neil |
| RESCUED: MOTHER AND BABY | Anne Fraser |

### *January*

| | |
|---|---|
| DARE SHE DATE THE DREAMY DOC? | Sarah Morgan |
| DR DROP-DEAD GORGEOUS | Emily Forbes |
| HER BROODING ITALIAN SURGEON | Fiona Lowe |
| A FATHER FOR BABY ROSE | Margaret Barker |
| NEUROSURGEON…AND MUM! | Kate Hardy |
| WEDDING IN DARLING DOWNS | Leah Martyn |

### *February*

| | |
|---|---|
| WISHING FOR A MIRACLE | Alison Roberts |
| THE MARRY-ME WISH | Alison Roberts |
| PRINCE CHARMING OF HARLEY STREET | Anne Fraser |
| THE HEART DOCTOR AND THE BABY | Lynne Marshall |
| THE SECRET DOCTOR | Joanna Neil |
| THE DOCTOR'S DOUBLE TROUBLE | Lucy Clark |

®™ MILLS & BOON®

# MEDICAL™

## Large Print

### *March*

| | |
|---|---|
| DATING THE MILLIONAIRE DOCTOR | Marion Lennox |
| ALESSANDRO AND THE CHEERY NANNY | Amy Andrews |
| VALENTINO'S PREGNANCY BOMBSHELL | Amy Andrews |
| A KNIGHT FOR NURSE HART | Laura Iding |
| A NURSE TO TAME THE PLAYBOY | Maggie Kingsley |
| VILLAGE MIDWIFE, BLUSHING BRIDE | Gill Sanderson |

### *April*

| | |
|---|---|
| BACHELOR OF THE BABY WARD | Meredith Webber |
| FAIRYTALE ON THE CHILDREN'S WARD | Meredith Webber |
| PLAYBOY UNDER THE MISTLETOE | Joanna Neil |
| OFFICER, SURGEON…GENTLEMAN! | Janice Lynn |
| MIDWIFE IN THE FAMILY WAY | Fiona McArthur |
| THEIR MARRIAGE MIRACLE | Sue MacKay |

### *May*

| | |
|---|---|
| DR ZINETTI'S SNOWKISSED BRIDE | Sarah Morgan |
| THE CHRISTMAS BABY BUMP | Lynne Marshall |
| CHRISTMAS IN BLUEBELL COVE | Abigail Gordon |
| THE VILLAGE NURSE'S HAPPY-EVER-AFTER | Abigail Gordon |
| THE MOST MAGICAL GIFT OF ALL | Fiona Lowe |
| CHRISTMAS MIRACLE: A FAMILY | Dianne Drake |

*Discover Pure Reading Pleasure with*

## Visit the Mills & Boon website for all the latest in romance

**Buy** all the latest releases, backlist and eBooks

**Find out** more about our authors and their books

**Join** our community and chat to authors and other readers

**Free** online reads from your favourite authors

**Win** with our fantastic online competitions

**Sign** up for our free monthly eNewsletter

**Tell us** what you think by signing up to our reader panel

**Rate** and review books with our star system

# www.millsandboon.co.uk

 Follow us at twitter.com/millsandboonuk

 Become a fan at facebook.com/romancehq